CW00848161

Eken Press Limited
87 Fore Street, Hertford,
Hertfordshire, SG14 1AL UK

Adventures in Thousandworld – The Darkenstar
© 2021 by Stevali Barn and Joseph A. Davis

First Edition
ISBN 978-1-908233-37-0

Translation: Joseph A. Davis
Illustrations: Yulia Ryabtseva
Cover Illustration: Therése Larsson, Tess of Sweden
Proofreading: Wendy Janes
Production and Graphic Design: Alan Maranik

Printed in Estonia by Print Best

All reproduction of text and images is prohibited without express
permission of the author or publisher.

Find out more about Joseph A. Davis
and his books at *trolyrien.com*.

Adventures in

THOUSANDWORLD

The Darkenstar

Joseph A. Davis

**EKEN
PRESS**

1

Julia realised that something about Kasir was off from the very moment the twelve-year-old refugee boy was presented to her class one chilly February morning. It wasn't his appearance, even if his broad, tanned face, his straight, black hair and his narrow brown eyes were rather unusual among the students in 6B. It wasn't his clothes, either, even if Julia thought they seemed a bit newer and nicer than they ought to be. It wasn't even the fact that he was a refugee – she knew a couple of girls from Syria in 6A, and Kasir wasn't like them at all. He wasn't like anyone else Julia had ever met. But it wasn't until April that she could finally put her finger on what was so different about him.

The school day began as normal: the quiet refugee boy sat drawing in his notebook as he ignored Ulf's maths lesson. As usual, Julia couldn't help but peek at the beautiful scene as it took form on the lined paper. *He's drawing too fast – he's sure to make a mistake,* she thought as a sketch of a palace with five towers rose up out of a meadow. The surrounding grass looked so realistic that Julia could almost feel it under her feet.

A garden with flowers and fountains grew around the palace as Kasir's pencil flew over the paper. Forests, lakes and mountains sprawled to the edges of the page. Closer to the palace, Kasir's pencil finally slowed as he drew a man and a woman dressed in long, beautiful garments. Their broad, smiling faces resembled Kasir's, and their hair was straight and dark like his. They stood holding hands at the centre of the drawing, even more beautiful than the exquisite scenery around them.

Julia realised she had once again let herself get distracted by Kasir. With a sigh, she turned her gaze to the whiteboard that Ulf was busy covering with numbers. She had just gathered that the lesson was about division when the sound of the refugee boy's pencil suddenly grew louder and quicker. Julia glanced back at his drawing and was horrified by what she saw. He was destroying the whole thing! His pencil quickened, and grey flames licked their way up the five towers. Thick, black smoke rose skyward.

"Stop it," Julia said quietly. The words came out a bit sharper than she'd intended, but then her feelings caught up with them, and her rising anger burned like the inferno that was destroying the lovely scene.

He drew too fast and made a mistake, she thought. *And now he's trying to hide it by destroying the whole drawing. He's trying to show how brilliant he is, tying to pretend that he never messes up.* Determined not to show that she cared, Julia sighed loudly. "Kasir, can't you stop scribbling and listen to the lesson instead?" she hissed. "You're never going to learn anything if you sit scribbling all the time." She was quite deliberate about using the word *scribbling*. If he was fishing for compliments, he wasn't going to get any from her.

As usual, Kasir didn't listen to her. He was completely engrossed in the destruction of his little fantasy world. The flames spread to the garden. The plumes of smoke grew, twisting into strange shapes, like dragons and nameless monsters made of black cloud. The looming figure of a giant grew out of the smoke, towering over the man and woman.

"I said stop it!" Julia whispered, a bit louder, as the smoky giant reached out with black tentacles and covered the lovely couple.

A drop of water appeared on the paper where the couple had disappeared. It gleamed in the sunlight that came slanting in through the classroom window. Julia looked at Kasir and discovered to her surprise that a tear was rolling down his cheek as he covered the entire drawing with black smoke. She forgot her irritation at once. "Kasir?" she said hesitantly.

"This is a maths lesson, not a chatting lesson," Ulf said in his stern voice. "Let's let each other focus!" He didn't say Julia's name and didn't even look at her, but everyone knew where his indignation was aimed. Her cheeks burned with humiliation as the teacher turned back to the board to write more numbers. A bubble of giggling swelled up in the corner where the horse girls sat, and Julia overheard the whispered words "Kasir" and "boyfriend", which made everything a thousand times worse. Of course Ulf didn't tell them off. He never told them off.

I'm just doing what Ulf told me to do, Julia thought bitterly as she pretended to be deeply fascinated by the numbers on the board. It was Ulf who had moved her to the desk beside Kasir's and asked her to help him – a job that was difficult and thankless enough even when she wasn't getting punished for doing it.

"Ulf," Tony, the class clown, said in an exaggerated whine. "Kasir's crying!"

Ulf whirled around to face Tony as if he intended to say something very stern. Then his gaze slipped to Kasir, and he hesitated. "Well, er … sometimes people cry – there's nothing wrong with that. But let's leave him in peace. Don't worry about him. Worry about yourself and the maths test. We're all going to have a reason to cry if we haven't learned this in time for the test." He tried to smooth things over with a smile, but it looked more like a strained grimace. No one laughed at his joke. Under normal circumstances, Julia would have laughed a little, purely to be kind, but not this time.

Ulf cleared his throat. "Anyway. As I was saying–"

At that moment, the fire alarm went off. Everyone jumped as the deafening wail pierced the relative silence of the maths lesson. Kasir looked up from his drawing and met Julia's gaze. His dark, gleaming eyes were wide with surprise. "What?" It was probably the first word he had said all day. He didn't pronounce it quite right – it sounded more like "Waath?" – but Julia understood what he meant.

"That's the fire alarm," Ulf explained hastily, approaching their desks. "It goes off if there's a fire – you know, flames, smoke – but this is probably only a test. It's not– Kasir, wait!"

But the boy had already risen from his chair at the word "smoke" and fled the classroom.

Julia stared at the doorway where Kasir had disappeared, mouth agape with shock. It wasn't just that he had run away so suddenly. It wasn't the strange fact that she had seen him draw a slender paintbrush from his pocket as he had leaped to his feet. What shocked her most was the thin plume of smoke she had seen trailing from the paintbrush's tip.

For a confused moment, Julia had the decidedly unpleasant feeling that the flames Kasir had drawn had somehow spread to the paintbrush and triggered the fire alarm. She shook her head. *I must be seeing things*, she thought. *I was looking at the drawing when I heard the alarm, and my eyes played a trick on me – that's all.* But the unpleasant feeling remained.

"All right, 6B!" Ulf shouted over the din of the fire alarm. "Let's get up nice and calmly and go to our assembly point in the playground."

"But Ulf, Kasir's run off!" Tony protested.

"Don't worry about him, Tony," Ulf said sternly. "You just worry about yourself. Everyone leave your things here," he added. "We're going straight out to the playground, quickly and quietly."

As chairs scraped on the floor and students rose to their feet, Ulf turned to Julia. "Could you go see if you can find Kasir? You know where we're supposed to gather. You can show him."

Julia tried to tell herself it was irritation with Kasir and Ulf that made her want to refuse. But her burning frustration had given way to a cold feeling writhing in the pit of her stomach.

She opened her mouth to say "no", but too late. Ulf had already moved on and was telling Tony off about something. Reluctantly, Julia rose to her feet. *I must have imagined it*, she told herself, trying hard to forget the image of the smoking paintbrush as she hurried out into the corridor.

2

Outside in the corridor, the piercing wail of the fire alarm mingled with the excited chatter of a crowd of year fours whose hapless teacher was trying to herd them toward the exit.

"Julia! Julia!"

Edvin's tousled shock of brown hair bounced up and down as he jumped in place among the other year fours. His blue eyes glittered cheerfully.

For a moment, Julia forgot Kasir's smoking paintbrush and groaned loudly. She had told Edvin never to talk to her at school. It was hard enough to fit in without a hyperactive little brother clinging to her all the time.

She pretended not to see him and hurried along the corridor in the opposite direction. But his shouting had already called unwanted attention to her.

"Julia!"

It was Manuela, Julia's art teacher, who was usually so happy to see her and her drawings. Now she looked anything but happy. "You're going the wrong way." The motherly woman's voice, with its exotic accent, was unusually firm.

"Ulf told me to find Kasir," Julia said, trying not to whine at her favourite teacher. This took quite some effort. It was so unfair that two different teachers would get cross with her because of Kasir on the same day!

Manuela's dark eyes narrowed. "I think Kasir can take care of himself," she said.

If only that were true! Julia thought. "Please, Manuela," she begged. "Ulf told me that I had to."

"Strange," said Manuela. "Very strange. But if you— Erik!" She turned to confront a large, blonde boy who had taken a small girl's mobile phone and was waving it over her head. The girl jumped and shrieked as if panicked at the thought of a gloomy, empty life without her precious phone.

She doesn't want to end up like me, Julia thought, taking the opportunity to flee. Mobile phones were one of the thousand things that Julia's mum had a firm opinion about. Like trendy clothes, riding lessons, trips to the cinema and everything else that all the other girls did. "It costs money," she would often say about such things. And she wondered why Julia sat in her room all the time, reading and drawing and never seeing any friends anymore.

Julia turned a corner and realised she should have asked Manuela if she had seen which direction Kasir had gone. Klippridge School was the largest school in the whole municipality, with two floors and a labyrinth of corridors. He could be anywhere. Maybe he had gone out to the playground with the others. The thought came almost as a comfort. Julia was not really sure that she wanted to meet Kasir alone at the moment.

But then she turned a corner and almost ran into him. The black-haired boy stood by a row of lockers, looking around in confusion at the crowd of students streaming past. This corridor was mostly year sixes, so the mass exodus was at least fairly orderly compared to the chaos of the year fours.

Kasir clutched his paintbrush in a white-knuckled grip. To Julia's relief, the brush looked completely ordinary, without a trace of smoke. It was in fact a very handsome brush, with a slender shaft of dark brown wood tipped with fine black hairs. *I must have imagined it*, she thought, breathing a sigh of relief.

"Come on, Kasir!" she said. "We have to go down to the playground and gather with the others."

The boy turned his confused gaze on her. "Smoke?" he said, gesturing quizzically with his free hand.

Julia's blood froze, and for a terrible moment she thought he was referring to his paintbrush. Then the wailing of the fire alarm pierced her thoughts and she shook off the ridiculous misunderstanding. "No, there's no smoke," she said. "And no fire, either. The school isn't burning, it's just a drill. It's pretend. We're supposed to go out to the playground and wait for them to tell us to come back in again."

"Pretend," Kasir said, seeming to understand at last. "Not smoke." The word smoke sounded strange coming from his mouth. He let out a small, relieved chuckle. Then he thrust the brush into his trouser pocket.

"Come on," Julia said. She remembered his earlier tears, and with a small degree of effort she managed to speak in a gentler tone. "We have to go out to the playground."

Kasir whistled a low note before nodding and following along. He had a strange habit of whistling quietly like that.

"You know, if you stopped whistling like that, people would stop teasing you for it," Julia said as she led him towards the stairs. "It isn't normal. You know, normal? If you want to fit in, you have to try to act like everyone else."

Kasir made no reply.

Julia felt a certain trepidation about art class after the fire drill. But as she entered the classroom, Manuela was her usual, cheerful self. She made no mention of Julia's earlier disappearance.

"Welcome, everyone!" Manuela said once all the year sixes had seated themselves at the long, black tables. As usual, Julia sat next to Kasir – but she was so relieved that Manuela wasn't cross with her that the seating arrangements hardly bothered her. In fact, she felt positively happy as she studied the coloured pencils, crayons, brushes and paints that lay waiting on the table. She loved to draw and paint. And she loved receiving praise from Manuela for her work.

"Today we're going to do something very special," the art teacher went on, holding up a manila folder. "As you all know, Easter is around the corner. Which means it's time for Klippsby's annual drawing competition."

Julia's heart leaped with joy. She had come in second place in year four and won the competition in year five. Which meant that last year, her winning drawing of a peacock hatching from a jewel-encrusted egg had been in the newspaper and hung in the library. She had received lots of praise from her teachers, and even the horse girls had been jealous of her for once. For her, the drawing competition was the high point of the school year.

"Easter?" Kasir said beside her. He spoke even slower than usual, as if trying to decide how the word tasted.

Julia's heart sank. A part of her wanted to tell him to forget the whole thing. Why couldn't he simply get lost in his drawing and ignore the teacher as usual? But then again, this was all about drawing.

At the front of the room, Manuela opened her folder and produced a number of photographs of birds and rabbits – large, beautiful close-ups. "You can study these and use them for inspiration," she said. "Your challenge this year is realism. If you want a challenge.

Otherwise you're free to draw as you please. But now you've made it all the way to year six, and since I know we have so many talented artists in the class …" Manuela smiled her special smile, the one that Julia loved to sun herself in. This time, the smile landed on Kasir.

It was as if a sudden thundercloud rose over Julia, blotting out the sun. *Why do all the grown-ups have to be like this with Kasir?* she thought. *He doesn't even care, and he never tries! Why is it always "poor Kasir"?*

Julia's mum had once said that Kasir must have experienced something terrible in his homeland – something so awful that he had been forced to flee to Sweden – and that must be why he hardly ever spoke. *But he's not the only one who's been through something terrible*, Julia thought. Her hand drifted to the ring that hung on a chain around her neck, the ring that was too large for her finger. As she felt its cool metal surface, a series of memories flashed through her mind: the smell of hospital, grown-ups dressed in black, the cold, echoing sanctuary of an old church. Suddenly she had forgotten all about Kasir and the drawing competition.

It wasn't until Manuela had finished speaking that Julia let go of the ring and came back to reality. She had a competition to win. She went to the front of the room and chose a particularly lovely picture of a toucan. If she could choose a bird that was prettier than Kasir's, maybe she would have a chance.

Maybe she could even convince him to choose an ugly photograph.

But Kasir didn't even bother to look at the photos. He just sat there drawing, in pencil as usual. It looked like he was working on a landscape. As Julia watched, rugged cliffs took shape around a small, round-topped hill. So far, the scene was hardly beautiful. Though it was very realistic, and that was the challenge.

Julia studied her toucan photo, considering the best way to capture the bird's bright colours. Should she try watercolour paints? Manuela loved watercolour, but it was a risky medium – so easy to make a mistake, and so hard to correct.

At last Julia decided to use coloured pencils and began selecting shades to match the exotic hues of the toucan's beak. Unfortunately, no pencil was quite perfect. But after a long debate with herself over two different shades of yellow-green, she had finally gathered some suitable colours.

As she reached past Kasir for a normal pencil to start sketching, her gaze fell on his drawing. It was very dark, with heavy black clouds reminiscent of the smoke monsters that had destroyed his previous drawing. Julia saw hints of wings, teeth, eyes and horns among the dark masses. The clouds, or monsters, darkened the entire sky – except for a single spot in the middle of the drawing, where a sunbeam broke through. The sun was nowhere to be seen; instead, the ray of light seemed to come from below, from something that looked like a letter T on the little round hill. Kasir whistled quietly to himself as he slowed down and worked on the T-shaped figure.

Soon it had become Jesus on the Cross, agonized and bleeding.

Julia breathed a sigh of relief. Kasir had missed the whole point. This was supposed to be an *Easter* picture, with cute, chubby chicks or cheerful rabbits, with flowers and sunshine and chocolate – not a dark, religious picture. They would never print something like that in the newspaper or hang it on the wall in the library.

"Oh my," Manuela said, appearing behind them and peering over Kasir's shoulder. Julia waited eagerly for her to say, "Well, I suppose that's one way to draw an Easter picture," or something else that would show how inappropriate the drawing was. But instead she praised the feeling that Kasir had captured. "You can almost feel his pain – but then that triumphant light! The contrast between the darkness and the light is wonderful. Have you come up with this picture on your own?"

"No, Manuela," Julia said quickly. For now she recognised the picture from the class's visit to the church the day before. The priest had stood and spoken about Easter in the vast, echoing sanctuary while the students had played quietly with their mobile phones. For once, Kasir had listened attentively. He had stared wide-eyed when the priest had pointed to a painting hanging on the wall and said something about "the light of the world". Julia vaguely remembered the man going on about the light "conquering the darkness" or something like that. Anyway, that painting had looked almost exactly like Kasir's drawing. Except for the clouds.

"It's from a painting," Julia explained. "We saw it yesterday, in the church."

"It must be a Maja Liljestrom," Manuela said. "And you're drawing it from memory?" She sounded deeply impressed.

Kasir didn't even bother to look up from his drawing. "Easter," he said quietly.

"And how is your picture coming along, Julia?" Manuela asked, shifting her gaze to the blank paper in front of Julia.

"Just fine, thanks," she replied. "The only problem is the colours. I can't seem to find any that are just right."

"Ah," the teacher said with a chuckle. "Well, there's precious little in this world that's just right. But I'm sure your drawing will be lovely." She patted Julia on the shoulder before proceeding to the next student.

3

"Julia! Time to wake up!"

Julia sighed and put her book facedown on her stomach. She had already been awake reading for two hours. There was nowhere she would rather be than here in her cosy bed with a good book or her drawing pad – except possibly the library. Today, the town square was at the very bottom of her list of places that sounded appealing. The adventure in her book was much more exciting than the boring ceremony in the square.

"Julia!" Her mother opened the door a crack. "Oh good, you're awake. Come down to breakfast. We have to hurry – we don't want to miss the excitement."

Julia groaned. "Can't I just lie here and read while you and Edvin go?"

"Oh, come on, Julia!"

Julia hated it when her mother said "Oh, come on, Julia!" For some reason, it seemed like she had been saying it constantly ever since Julia had started year six.

"This is both art and local history," her mother continued. "And a little bit of sunlight and fresh air wouldn't hurt you."

Julia's mother never thought that a little bit of sunlight or fresh air would hurt anyone. That was what she said whenever she made them bike somewhere instead of taking the car. Julia's thoughts drifted to the book she was reading. The protagonist, the thief Rapp Galacto, was steering his spaceship right into the sun. If Julia's mother had been on the bridge, she probably would have said "A little bit of sunlight and fresh air won't hurt" right before they crashed into the sun and were obliterated. And if Julia were piloting the ship, she would probably add an "Oh, come on, Julia!" Julia giggled.

"I'm glad you're so bright and cheery," her mother said. "Maybe you can help cheer up your friend Kasir."

"Kasir?" Julia sat up in a sudden panic. "What does he have to do with anything?"

"Eva asked me if we could bring him along with us today. She recently became his guardian, after the last one quit."

"Mum, you have to say no! Seriously!"

"Oh, come on, Julia! He's been through so much."

"He's not the only one!" Julia's gaze landed on the framed photograph of her father, beside the battered pony book on her bedside table. "Mum, you have to say no! I can't deal with him today!"

"I'm sorry, Julia, but …" That was also something her mother said all too often. This time she finished with, "… they're already on their way."

"On their way here?" Julia cried. "Are they coming here?" She leaped up out of bed and rushed to the bathroom. This was a nightmare. Kasir must not under any circumstances be allowed to enter her house. He must not be allowed to see how small it was, how everything was broken, how they didn't have all the fun things that everyone else had. And under no circumstances could he be allowed to see her in the old, worn out pony pyjamas she had grown out of ages ago.

The door to the bathroom was locked. "Edvin!" Julia shouted, pounding on the door. "I have to shower!"

"Okay, just wait a minute," he said. Julia heard a page turn.

"You can read your comic book on the couch!" she said. "I have to use the shower now! You have thirty seconds!"

"It sounds like someone wants to be nice and fresh and smartly dressed for Kasir," her mother said with a little laugh.

At that moment, Julia wished that her mother really had crashed into the sun in a spaceship. And that she herself had also been obliterated in the same crash.

Her mother hummed cheerfully as she slipped past Julia towards the kitchen to prepare the porridge.

After what felt like an eternity, Edvin flushed and opened the door. Julia didn't even bother to tell him to wash his hands – she just rushed in and closed the door behind her. The mirror confirmed what she had feared: her hair looked even more atrocious than her pyjamas. She was usually proud that she had inherited her father's wild brown hair, just like Edvin. But that was after she had washed and dried and brushed it. Now she wished she had inherited her mother's straight blonde hair instead.

Julia got ready faster than she had ever done before. But it wasn't fast enough. She heard the front door open, and then the sound of her mother and Eva falling into a bottomless pit of chatter. Those two could chat for an eternity without ever tiring. And since the bathroom door, the front door and the stairs were all right next to each other in their cramped little house, Julia had no chance of sneaking up to her room without being seen.

She looked at her pyjamas and bitterly regretted that she had not thought to bring a change of clothes with her into the bathroom.

"Julia!" her mother shouted. "Your friend Kasir is here!"

"I'm almost ready, Mum!" Julia shouted. "You can start without me!" But she took her time drying and brushing her hair. She waited until she was certain that Eva had left and the others had gone into the kitchen.

Then she wrapped herself in her towel – better that than the pink pony pyjamas – opened the door and sprinted up to her room as fast as she could. There she considered putting on the pretty yellow spring dress that her aunt had bought for her twelfth birthday. But then she remembered her mother's comment about wanting to be smartly dressed for Kasir and chose blue jeans and a T-shirt instead. Also presents from her aunt.

When she arrived at the breakfast table, Edvin was busy doing his card trick for Kasir. "Is *this* your card?" he asked, proudly displaying a five of spades.

Kasir nodded and whistled quietly.

Edvin imitated his whistle almost perfectly. He was good at whistling, as their mother said that their father had been. Julia couldn't remember ever hearing Dad whistle, but she had only been six years old when he had passed away. Edvin, on the other hand, she had heard thousands of times – and it got on her nerves.

But when Kasir heard Edvin's whistle, he brightened, suddenly happier than Julia had ever seen him. He smiled and laughed, slapped Edvin on the shoulder and whistled another tone.

When Edvin saw his excited gesture, he copied that tone as well, and Kasir laughed and clapped his hands.

"That's enough!"

Julia was shocked by the vehemence in her mother's voice. Mum shook her head as if she was a bit taken aback herself. "Stop copying him, Edvin. It's not polite."

"But Mum, he thinks it's fun!" Edvin protested.

"No, I've said that's enough. Eat your porridge." Their mother turned to Kasir and addressed him in a gentler tone, as if she were ashamed of her outburst. "Congratulations on winning the competition. I saw your drawing in the newspaper. You really are talented."

Kasir nodded and whistled quietly.

"You should say thanks," said Edvin. "That's what we say here in Sweden."

"Thanks," Kasir said quietly without lifting his gaze from the tabletop.

"I see that you and Eva rode your bikes," Julia's mother said. "I hope you feel all right about biking to the square."

Julia groaned.

It was Julia's turn to do the washing up after breakfast, but that was fine with her. Rather that than be with Kasir. She just wished her mother hadn't insisted on showing him the whole house.

When she had finished with the dishes, it was time to get the bikes out. Thankfully, Kasir's bike wasn't too much nicer than hers. Though it was a bit bigger, almost exactly the right size for him. He was slightly shorter than Julia, but her bike looked like a little girl's toy next to his.

Julia had plenty of time to study his bicycle as she pedaled slowly so as not to have to talk with him. He seemed a bit unused to biking and had a hard time getting started again each time they stopped at a junction. And although Edvin showed him plenty of tricks and challenged him to try them, he just pedalled straight on ahead, wobbling a bit from side to side.

As Julia pedalled behind Kasir, she tried not to stare at the paintbrush sticking up out of his pocket – the same brush he had taken out during the fire drill a few days ago. She suppressed the unpleasant feeling that it awoke in her and tried just to be irritated with Kasir instead. *Why does he have to bring that along?* she thought. *Can't he stop showing off for one second? Does he have to let everyone know that he's the great artist, the proud winner of the drawing competition?* She thought bitterly about how her picture hadn't made it into the newspaper this year. *That picture of Jesus was completely inappropriate*, she thought. *If all the grown-ups didn't feel so bad for Kasir, they would never have chosen it. If I had drawn it, they would have told me it didn't fit the theme of Easter. He didn't even colour it!*

She tried to focus on her frustration as they approached the square. For a while, she managed to forget the lingering dread that the brush inspired in her.

They were among the first people to arrive at the town's bicentennial celebration. That suited Julia just fine, because it meant that relatively few people saw her park her small, beat-up bike. It also meant that she got to see the drama playing out between the arrangers of the event and the Troubadour, Klippsby's most notorious resident, as they tried to remove him from the premises.

4

Julia didn't know why the large, middle-aged man was called the Troubadour. She had never seen him sing or play any instrument. He usually just sat on a bench in the park or in the square in his ragged brown coat, whistling at passers-by. When she had walked past him in her new yellow dress on the day of her birthday picnic, he had whistled at her. Her mother had been livid and given Julia a lecture about how the man was a drunk and how it wasn't safe to talk to him. As if she didn't already know.

Now the Troubadour sat on the low marble pedestal where *The Unlucky Hand* stood. The bronze sculpture's proper name was actually *Welcome*. Julia's mother had worked in the art museum once upon a time before she had become unemployed and then cashier at the supermarket, and she had made sure that Julia learned the proper names of every single one of Klippsby's peculiar statues. Julia had learned that *Welcome* was the work of Angelica Skogsbergh, the city's great sculptor who had filled Klippsby with her incomprehensible art some time before Julia had been born. But most people called this sculpture, which stood in the very centre of the square, *The Unlucky Hand*, and they didn't bother about who had created it. It was, after all, a hand, with an upturned palm and fingers slightly bent, large enough for two teenagers to sit in and snog or for five children to climb on at a time. And the hole going straight through the centre of its palm showed that the hand's owner must have suffered some unfortunate accident. Some children called it *The Clumsy Carpenter's Hand*. Maybe because the woodwork teacher at Klippridge School called it that – he tended to use it as a warning example.

Today there weren't any children playing on *Welcome*. No one dared while the Troubadour sat on the pedestal, turned toward the new sculpture that stood waiting to be unveiled about four metres away. He certainly looked frightening, with his puffy red face, his unkempt grey beard and his long, foul-smelling brown coat. He was the kind of person one was happy to avoid. But now he had sat himself right in the middle of the action. Therefore, something had to be done about him.

This heavy responsibility fell on the shoulders of Hans Karlfeldt, the man who always gave speeches on Walpurgis Eve and every other occasion when the town needed a speech. He was an important person in some way, even if Julia had never really understood what he had done to deserve it. Perhaps he was just elegant and well-dressed.

While Julia's mother remained behind at the bike rack, chatting with another woman, Julia stood at a safe distance and watched Hans Karlfeldt's attempt to shoo the Troubadour away from *Welcome*.

The tall man with his well-trimmed grey goatee and his fine suit approached the slumping, heavyset vagrant with determined steps. "Excuse me," he said. "We're going to have an unveiling ceremony here soon."

"Generosity," said the Troubadour. He had a habit of speaking a bit incoherently. "I wouldn't miss it, Hansy boy." He took a gulp from the bottle he had with him.

Hans Karlfeldt stared, mouth agape. It was quite entertaining to see.

"This is a great day," the Troubadour continued. "A day for celebration, wouldn't you say? Shall we have a toast?" He held out his half-empty bottle.

Hans Karlfeldt cleared his throat and adjusted his tie. "The speech is to be held here, between the sculptures," he said.

"Is that right?" said the Troubadour. "And who will be speaking about Angelica's work today? Some expert, I suppose? A great artist or academic? Or maybe someone who knew her well?"

Now Hans Karlfeldt raised his voice. "Professor Modéus," he said. "Would you kindly vacate this sculpture so that the ceremony may commence?"

Julia didn't know why the smartly dressed man chose to call the Troubadour *Professor Modéus*, but it sounded like some kind of ironic insult. She almost felt bad for the Troubadour. But then the man rose with a look in his eyes like a gathering thunderstorm. He was a large man, as tall as Hans Karlfeldt but perhaps twice as wide under his filthy coat. For a moment, Julia thought he was going to punch the other man in the face.

Hans Karlfeldt looked just as angry, and the two men stood glaring at each other. Then the Troubadour lowered his gaze, whistled quietly and loped off to sit on a bench at the edge of the square.

"Well done, Hans," another man said, patting Hans Karlfeldt on the shoulder.

Julia hastily looked away before the Troubadour could look up and catch her staring. She quickly surveyed the square in search of someone to talk to. Her brother had run off to the ice-cream stand, her mother was still engrossed in conversation with the woman by the bike rack, and Kasir …

Kasir was headed straight towards the bench where the Troubadour sat hanging his head. As Julia watched in horror, the boy whistled three notes that almost sounded like a question, drew the paintbrush from his back pocket and held it out as if he wanted the vagrant to take it.

The Troubadour leaped to his feet. Without thinking, Julia rushed forward to rescue Kasir.

"Kasir!" she hissed, pulling the boy away. "Come on. Let's leave him in peace."

The Troubadour towered over them. His face was frightful to see, with large, staring eyes. He looked as if he had gone completely mad.

Kasir struggled with Julia and held out the paintbrush again. He whistled the same three notes.

With a wordless cry, the Troubadour turned and fled the square. "Forgive me, Angelica!" he wailed as he ran. "I tried." Soon he had disappeared behind the corner of the off license.

Julia's mother came hurrying to the children. "Are you all right?" she asked. She placed a hand on Julia's shoulder and looked into her eyes, then repeated the same procedure with Kasir. "Did he say anything to you? Did he hurt you?"

"Wow!" Edvin said, appearing behind Julia. "Kasir, you scared off the Troubadour! You've saved the day!"

Kasir didn't seem to understand any of this. He stood with his paintbrush in his outstretched hand, staring at the corner where the Troubadour had disappeared. For a moment, Julia was almost afraid that he meant to follow him.

"Are you all right?" her mother continued.

"Yes, yes, we're fine, Mum," Julia said with an exasperated sigh. "You don't have to ask us a thousand times!"

Out of the corner of her eye, she saw Caroline and Elin, two of the horse girls, in their fashionable clothes. They stood by the ice-cream stand, and they had their eyes on her.

Oh no, Julia thought, wishing the earth would open up and swallow her. *Did they see what happened with the Troubadour? Are they going to talk?* Of course they were going to talk. And Julia didn't know which would be worse – if they talked about her as if she were friends with the Troubadour, or if they talked about Kasir as if he were the hero who had chased the man away.

Mercifully, the ceremony eventually began, and by that time so many people had gathered, Julia was able to hide herself in the crowd.

Hans Karlfeldt stood between the two sculptures, with *The Unlucky Hand* on his left and the new, hulking shape hidden under a white cloth on his right. He tested his microphone. When he was finally satisfied with the sound quality, he began a long, solemn speech about Klippsby, their beloved hometown. He spoke about how Klippsby had been a haven for the arts from the very beginning, ever since the days when the Klippstream Colourists had painted in their cottages out in the woods. He spoke about how much the arts had meant to the town and about all the great artists who had lived there over the course of Klippsby's two-hundred-year history.

It was a very dull speech, and after a few minutes, Edvin wandered off to look in the shop windows. Kasir, on the other hand, stayed right where he was and stared – but not at Hans Karlfeldt. Instead, he seemed to be studying *The Unlucky Hand* intently.

His behaviour irritated Julia, but not as much as the paintbrush sticking up out of his back pocket. The fact that he had tried to give it to the Troubadour, and that the Troubadour had then fled, gnawed at Julia's thoughts. She tried to think about something else, anything, and her thoughts landed on the book she was reading at home. The hero, Rapp Galacto, had started off as a pickpocket. And he had humiliated the arrogant general Riff Torum by stealing the power wand from his belt in the middle of a conversation, while the general was busy calling him a simple thief.

Julia looked around to make sure no one was watching. Her mother had her eyes on Hans Karlfeldt and seemed captivated by his every word. And Edvin was off by the toy shop, staring at whatever new toys were being displayed in the window. Their mother would never buy any of it for him, but maybe he would manage to convince their aunt the next time she came to visit.

Stealing from a refugee is a horrible thing to do, a voice inside Julia whispered.

True, she answered the voice, *but I'm going to give the brush back tomorrow. I'm just going to …* But her thought was so ridiculous that she didn't even want to admit having it, not even to herself. Really, there was no reason to inspect the paintbrush – what could it be, other than an ordinary brush? *No, I just want to teach Kasir a lesson*, she thought. *Show him he can't show off his brush like some great artist after winning the drawing competition so unfairly.*

Silently she approached the refugee boy. She would have to act quickly. She reached out her hand, but then she hesitated. Was she turning into a bully like Tony at school? But then she remembered Kasir's infuriating, inappropriate drawing in the newspaper. Her hand shot out, and her fingers closed on the brush.

As she touched the smooth wooden handle, something like an electric shock ran through her hand. Thankfully she managed not to cry out.

That's not all that strange, she thought, backing silently away and slipping the brush into her own pocket. *It's the same thing that happens when Edvin walks on the carpet at home with his fuzzy slippers and gives me a shock on the ear. Nothing strange at all.* The brush was too long to go all the way down into her pocket. She moved it to the other pocket, as far away from Kasir as possible.

"And so," Hans Karlfeldt was saying, "it is my great honour and privilege to show you Angelica Skogsbergh's masterpiece … *Generosity!*" He drew back the white cloth with a flourish, revealing a large sculpture in weathered bronze.

It was another hand, almost exactly like the first. A mirror image of *The Unlucky Hand*.

A confused murmur went through the crowd. Kasir leaped for joy, whistling and shouting aloud in a language Julia did not understand. She backed away a few more steps with the brush in her pocket.

Eva called Julia's mother later that day. Apparently Kasir had lost something – she thought it must be something very important to him, but she couldn't get him to explain what it was. He had refused to go home and insisted on biking straight back to the square. Even

as Eva spoke, he was still searching there. She wondered if anyone in Julia's family had seen anything – if Kasir might have forgotten something at their house.

"Julia?" Her mother looked up from the phone. Julia had been sitting at the kitchen table listening to the entire conversation as she pretended to do her homework.

She sighed. "Mum, how should I know if he's lost something here, if I don't even know what it is?" She closed her maths book and marched off to her bedroom with heavy steps. There she closed the door behind her and took a deep breath. An unpleasant feeling was growing in the pit of her stomach.

I should have said something, she thought. *Everyone would have thought I was so kind, if I just found his lost brush so he could stop searching and go home.* But now it was too late. She had made her decision. *I'm going to give it back tomorrow anyways*, she reminded herself. *I don't have to say that I took it from his pocket. I can say I found it on the road on the way to school – like it just fell out of his pocket while we were biking.*

She cast a sideways glance at her pencil case. Should she finally take the brush out and inspect it properly? But now the whole thing felt ridiculous. *It was just my imagination*, she thought. *And now I've stolen from a refugee.*

She opened her maths book again to give herself something else to think about. After a while she gave up and dug out her book about Rapp Galacto. But somehow, reading about a thief did little to raise her spirits.

5

That evening, Julia's mother was unexpectedly called in to work at the supermarket. So Julia was left to make dinner for herself and Edvin. As usual when they were home alone, he was completely impossible. He complained and whined when she told him to do the washing up after dinner, and when she tried to get him to go to bed, he protested that he should get to stay up as late as her. "It's Easter break," he whined.

"You're only ten, and I'll be thirteen soon," said Julia. "And you know that Mum wants us to get our sleep. I'm going straight to bed as soon as you've settled down."

But when her little brother had gone to bed, she took out her drawing pad and her pencil case and settled down at the kitchen table to draw. She had to do something to try to calm her nerves after all the stress about Kasir and Edvin.

Julia opened the pencil case and was just about to select a pencil when her gaze fell on the fine, dark brown handle of the brush she had hidden there. Why did Kasir have to get so upset about such a small thing? It was a rather nice brush, but she had never even seen him use it to paint anything. Why go back to the square to look for it? Why not just buy a new brush?

Julia shifted in her seat and became aware of the cool touch of the ring against her collarbone. Her father's ring. If she lost it, would she just buy a new one?

In her thoughts, she groped for the last happy memory she had of her father. Julia, then a sleepy six-year-old, had lain in bed listening while he had read from the old pony book and performed all the voices. She still read it now and then when she had a hard time sleeping. Sometimes she even thought she could remember how all the voices had sounded. Sometimes she couldn't remember, which hurt terribly.

Could the brush be something that Kasir remembered his parents by?

I'll have to apologise when I give it back to him tomorrow, Julia thought. *Not for taking it – he can't ever find out about that. I'll say I found it and apologise for not recognising it and giving it back to him right away.*

She reached out her hand to take the slender brush. Then she remembered the shock she had experienced in the square and hesitated. *Don't be ridiculous,* she chided herself and took a firm hold of the brush. No shock.

The dark wooden handle was soft and smooth. A sudden impulse made her raise the brush to her nose – perhaps to check if it smelled of smoke? But of course it didn't. It was probably just the late hour that gave her such strange thoughts. Instead she detected a faint spicy odour. Was it made of some rare wood? Something that only grew in Kasir's homeland?

She felt the brush's tickling softness against the palm of her hand. Then she pressed harder and saw how the silky bristles spread out against her skin. When she pulled the brush back, a small grey spot remained on her palm.

Typical, she thought. She laid the brush down on the table and went to the tap to wash her hand. *He cares about the brush so much but can't be bothered to clean it properly. Boys.*

The cold water failed to rinse the grey spot away. Julia soaped up her palm and tried again, with the same result. *How irritating*, she thought as she scrubbed her skin with a wet cloth. At last the spot disappeared. But now the cloth was completely grey.

She stared at the discoloured cloth, and her thoughts drifted to the smoke monsters that Kasir had drawn a few days ago – the monsters that had destroyed the palace and the whole little world he had created.

A movement in the corner of Julia's eye made her jump. She turned toward the kitchen table. Had something moved in the darkness outside the window?

It was only a bird or something, she told herself. With some mental effort, she forced herself to return to her seat at the table and resume drawing. She chose a pencil and began sketching a horse – the kind of horse she had longed to ride ever since Caroline and Elin had got their horses in year five and stopped spending time with her. But just like her friendship with them, her drawing couldn't seem to go quite right. She was forced to erase several times, and the eraser left grey splotches that once again made her think of Kasir's smoke monsters.

As she worked on her drawing, she shifted in her seat, unconsciously scooting further and further away from the dark window. Several times she thought she saw movement out of the corner of her eye, but she told herself she must be imagining things. It was probably just a tree waving in the breeze. She kept her gaze locked on the paper, afraid of what she might see in the darkness outside if she looked too closely.

A clicking, rattling sound at the front door made Julia jump. The door opened with a creak.

"Mum?" Julia said. She cast a glance at the clock: 10.45. Her mother was supposed to work until eleven.

Footsteps approached in the hall, and Julia rose from her chair. "Mum?"

A short, dark figure came around the corner into the kitchen, and Julia screamed.

It was Kasir. The boy strode into the kitchen and approached Julia silently, with a determined look in his eyes.

"Kasir?" Julia said, her voice thin with panic as she backed away.

The boy drew closer, and every evil rumour Julia had ever heard about refugees and violence, everything her mother had told her not to believe, flashed through her mind. *He's come here to murder me*, she thought, horrified, as the window-ledge pressed into her back. She was cornered.

With a sudden, violent motion, Kasir lunged. Julia raised her hands to defend herself, screaming.

But Kasir wasn't going for her. He snatched the dark brown brush from the table and then whirled around to face the hallway, holding the brush out before him like a little sword. "Not safe," he said without casting a backward glance at Julia. "Smoke."

Julia's fear melted away in a sudden wave of burning anger. "What's this about, Kasir?" she demanded. "You can't break into people's houses in the middle of the night without knocking! I don't know what you're used to where you come from, but here …"

Something moved in the doorway, and the refugee boy charged with his paintbrush raised and ready to strike.

"Easy there!" Edvin said, retreating back into the hallway. "Kasir, what are you doing here? I was sleeping, and I heard a scream and …"

Kasir lowered his brush and shoved Edvin toward the front door. "Not safe … smoke."

Now Julia's rage boiled over. "Don't touch my little brother!" she roared, charging out into the hallway. "If you—"

Edvin shrieked. His face was pale, and his eyes were as wide as saucers.

Julia turned to see what her little brother was staring at – and caught sight of a dark, hulking shape in the darkened living room. The shape was moving, and it clearly wasn't human.

6

At first glance, the figure looked like a dark cross between a misshapen squid and a troll out of a book of fairy tales. When it turned to fix its eyeless gaze on Julia, all of its contours blurred and twisted in the air like smoke. *A nightmare*, she thought, terrified, as the monster slowly approached her. *This is a nightmare.*

"Run!" Kasir shouted, pushing his way past Julia and placing himself between her and the monster. He raised his paintbrush, whistled sharply at the smoky creature and began painting in the air with rapid, frantic movements.

The monster froze, its dark tentacles waving languidly as if moved by an underwater current or a breeze that only it felt. Kasir roared and struck the air with his brush. Something like a net of light grey smoke flew out of the brush, towards the monster – and broke over the dark creature with no visible effect. The monster let out a terrible, rhythmic coughing sound, like a parody of laughter. Then it came gliding towards them.

"Run!" Kasir cried, shoving Julia and Edvin towards the door.

Julia snapped out of her shock and fled out into the darkness along with the two boys. It was only once they had traversed about half the length of street that she realised she was running in her socks. She glanced over her shoulder and saw the dark monster come streaming out through the door like smoke. Another creature, similar but larger and more terrible than the first, sat on the roof of the house, and several smaller smoke monsters hovered in mid-air over the trees. Going back to get her shoes was out of the question. She redoubled her speed, quickly catching up with the others.

"Here!" Kasir said, cutting across a lawn.

"Wait," Julia said, stopping at the edge of the grass. "We have to get to the supermarket to find our mum." *And what's Mum supposed to do about this?* she thought. But she was so frightened that she hardly knew what she was saying.

"No, here!" Kasir insisted.

Julia turned and saw several dark shapes come gliding through the night air. Then she ran in the direction Kasir wanted, pulling Edvin along with her.

"Julia," Edvin said, panicked. "Is this for real?"

"No," Julia replied. "It's just a dream. But don't stop running." She wished that someone would say the same thing to her.

As they ran, Julia became conscious of the night chill and wished she had brought her jacket with her. But her shoes would have been even better. She tried to relieve the pain in her feet by running on the narrow strip of grass between the pavement and the road – but the grass was damp and cold. At least she hadn't changed into her pony pyjamas. Edvin ran in his night clothes, a pair of shorts and a large T-shirt with the supermarket's logo on it – one of their mother's old work shirts. Julia would have felt quite embarrassed if the situation hadn't been so urgent and absurd. Thankfully no one was out.

"What are those *things*?" she asked Kasir as they crossed the bridge towards the town centre.

"Danger," the boy answered. "Run. Not stop."

Julia glanced over her shoulder and saw something dark moving through the air on the other side of the bridge. The creatures had not given up the chase.

"Hurry up," she said to her brother.

"But my feet hurt," he complained.

"I know," Julia said. "But we have to run!"

But where? The refugee boy was leading them towards the middle of town, but was there really any safety from the smoky monsters there?

"Kasir!" she panted as they ran. "Where are we going? What are we going to do?"

Kasir did not answer.

Soon they arrived at Klippsby's small high street. There were lights in a few shop windows, but nothing was open except the pub on Main Street. The sound of conversation and laughter echoed over the cobblestone streets, the only sound in the otherwise deserted town centre.

Kasir led them towards the pub, and at first Julia thought they were going to stop there. Would they be safe in there among the grown-ups? But the refugee boy ran right past the place, and Julia and Edvin followed.

They ran out into the square, and Kasir led them towards the two great bronze hands at its centre.

Something moved there in the shadows, and to Julia's horror, a large, dark shape rose between the hands and turned toward them. She grabbed hold of Edvin's arm and stopped short.

Kasir approached the dark figure with hurried steps, whistling and babbling unintelligibly.

"No, leave me alone!" the figure answered with a note of panic in his voice, lurching away from the refugee boy. At once Julia recognised the Troubadour.

Kasir continued babbling and whistling. "Please," he said at last. "We need …" He held out his brush in the darkness, just as he had done before, at the ceremony.

The Troubadour turned and whistled a sharp tone that made Kasir take a step back. "Don't you understand, boy? I don't do that kind of thing anymore … I can't. You've come to the wrong person. You need Angelica, not me." His voice was thick with barely suppressed tears.

Kasir grabbed hold of the sleeve of the Troubadour's coat. "Please! Not wrong! Not wrong."

"Julia?"

Julia heard the terror in her little brother's voice and turned around. A dark shape was approaching them, hovering over the rooftops like a deformed, four-winged bird made of black smoke.

"Kasir!" Julia cried, pointing. She backed towards Kasir, pulling her little brother along with her.

The refugee boy released the vagrant, pointed his brush at the smoke monster and started painting. A large, light grey bird shape flew from his brush and rushed at the shadowy monster.

The two winged creatures fought in the air for a moment, and then both vanished.

"You did it!" Edvin exclaimed, slapping Kasir on the back. "You did it, Kasir!"

But then several more dark bird shapes rose over the rooftops. Some were four-winged like the first. Others were more butterfly-shaped, with two large, round wings. There were over a dozen of them, all headed straight for the town square.

Kasir whistled in panic and hurled another light grey bird at the approaching monsters. "Please," he said, pressing the brush into the Troubadour's hand.

The towering vagrant looked down at the brush. Then, to Julia's surprise, he turned his gaze to her and sighed deeply. "I'll do this one last time, Angelica," he said. "For Henrik's daughter."

How does he know Dad's name? Julia wondered as the Troubadour began painting in the air.

A swarm of small, light grey butterflies fluttered out of the brush. They encircled the two great bronze hands like a light grey cloud.

The enormous black bird creatures hesitated just beyond the cloud of butterflies. "Come on," said the Troubadour, shaking his fist at them. "Come and take me, too! Come and finish what you started!"

The black monsters screeched – a sound that Julia was certain would haunt her dreams if she survived this. Then they flew straight into the cloud.

The light grey butterflies attacked the dark creatures. The smoky monsters fell to the ground and writhed on the cobblestones, completely covered in small, light grey wings. Julia leaped aside as one of them almost touched her foot with an arm like a plume of smoke – but then the monster dissolved and vanished.

Soon there were only light grey butterflies left. Then the Troubadour drew in the air again, and they disappeared as well.

"It's done," the Troubadour panted, trying to give the brush back to the boy. "I don't know how they got here or what they were after, and I don't want to know. But you have to be more careful from now on, because …"

The refugee boy refused to take the brush. He whistled several terrified tones and pointed towards the off license. A creature like a giant squid came half-gliding, half-shuffling around the corner towards them.

The Troubadour cursed. "Do you have anything stronger than this brush, boy?"

Kasir whistled two low tones.

The Troubadour cursed again and turned to the enormous bronze hands. He painted some hasty symbols on *Welcome*. "Grab the sculpture and hold on," he said.

"Troubadour, it's coming!" Edvin said, terrified. The squid-like monster seemed to pick up speed as it glided closer and closer.

"Put your hands on the sculpture!" the Troubadour ordered. "No time for discussion! I have to save you!"

Kasir took hold of *Welcome*'s colossal pointer finger and nodded to Julia. She shoved Edvin toward the statue, and they took a finger each.

Meanwhile, the great smoky creature came gliding toward them. *Is it going to hurt?* Julia wondered anxiously. *But in a nightmare, I shouldn't be able to feel anything, right?*

The squid-like monster glided up to the sculpture and reached for them with tentacles of dark, oily smoke.

Then the world dissolved into black.

7

"This is all wrong."

Julia blinked. It was the Troubadour who had spoken, and now the huge man stood staring doubtfully at the tall, slender tree trunks that surrounded them in the darkness. Julia felt soft, cool earth through her socks.

The Troubadour turned, and Julia followed his gaze and saw a large, dark ball on a pedestal. "This is the right portal stone," he muttered. "But the place is all wrong." He lifted his eyes to the treetops. "Why is it night here?"

"Why wouldn't it be night here?" asked Edvin. "It was night in the square. And where is *here* anyway? This is the weirdest dream ever! I want to wake up!"

Julia laid a hand on her little brother's shoulder, in part to comfort him and in part to get him to be quiet. The Troubadour was dangerous – maybe even more dangerous than she had realised.

"It's never night here," the man muttered, ignoring the boy's other question. "Or rather, it never *was* night here – maybe she's changed style."

Kasir whistled something quietly.

"What do you mean, 'who'?" the Troubadour shot back in an offended tone. He fixed the refugee boy with a stern gaze. "Who are you to ask me questions? This whole mess is your fault! I don't know who you are or what you were doing in our world, but I'm not stupid. Those darkenwraiths didn't come to admire the sculptures – they were after you!"

Something in the Troubadour's tone and Kasir's terrified expression made Julia defy her own fear and step forward between them. "They were after *us*," she corrected. "Don't be so hard on him. It's not his fault."

"Oh, you don't think so?" The Troubadour laughed bitterly. "Little girl, you have no idea how serious this is. Maybe I don't either. But come on. I've been dragged into this now, but not for long. This'll be the last time for me. As soon as I've turned you over to her, I'm going home to see how much wine it takes to forget all of this. Wait, I just need to get my bearings." He turned and studied the globe. "None of you happen to have a mobile phone you could shine over here?"

Now Julia's fear gave way to her anger. "My name isn't little girl," she said. "And I don't know why we should trust you or follow you anywhere. If you're the one who's brought us here, that makes you a kidnapper!"

"He saved us from those … *things*," Edvin pointed out.

"Darkenwraiths," the Troubadour said, groping over the globe's smooth surface with his left hand. In his right, he clutched Kasir's paintbrush. "That's probably the best translation of their name. But do you mean to tell me that none of you has a mobile phone? Come on, every child has one these days."

"Not every child," said Julia.

"There's no guarantee it would have worked here anyway," the Troubadour muttered. He seemed to find what he was looking for on the globe and straightened up. "This way!" he said, turning around and plunging into the forest.

Kasir followed, and Edvin was about to do the same when Julia grabbed hold of his arm. "Wait," she said.

The Troubadour spun around furiously. "We don't have time for this right now, little miss!" he snapped.

Julia drew herself up to her full height. "My name isn't little miss either," she said. "And my brother and I don't intend to follow you until you explain why you've brought us here, who you plan to turn us over to and why."

"He saved our lives," Edvin pointed out again.

The Troubadour heaved a great sigh. "All right then, *Julia*," he said. "Let me put this succinctly. This boy has got you and your little brother Edvin into serious trouble. Now he's also dragged me into it even though none of this is my problem and I really can't deal with any of it. Really, I would like to leave the three of you here in the forest and hope that the darkenwraiths find your friend and forget all about our world, but I owe your dad a favour. So I'm going to turn you over to Maja, who's a whole lot nicer than I am – maybe even nice enough to help you. Is that enough of an explanation? Can we hurry now, little miss, before the darkenwraiths find some way to catch up with us?"

Julia blinked.

Kasir took hold of her arm. "Hurry," he said. "Not safe."

"He saved our lives," Edvin pointed out for the third time. "And it sounds like he was friends with Dad."

Julia looked at the large, foul-smelling drunkard and thought of the framed photo on her bedside table: a strong, kind man, determined and intelligent and perfect. "Just because he says he owes Dad a favour doesn't mean they were friends," she said firmly. "Lots of good people help alcoholics."

It wasn't a particularly kind thing to say, and she knew it. But this whole situation made her feel confused and powerless and frightened, which made her angry.

The Troubadour muttered something and loped off into the darkness of the forest. After a moment's hesitation, Julia followed.

"This dream feels so *real*," Edvin said, jogging along beside her. "My feet feel sort of ... *dirty*, and everything smells so, so ..."

"I know," said Julia. She felt the cool, damp earth through her socks, and the smell of soil and forest and decomposing leaves was thoroughly convincing. She was starting to fear that this might not be a dream.

"Do you understand any of this?" she asked, turning to Kasir.

For a while, she heard only their footsteps in the soft dirt and the whispering breeze in the treetops. "Maybe," the refugee boy said at last.

"Could you hurry up?" the Troubadour complained ahead of them.

Julia didn't answer. She didn't hurry either. It was bad enough running like mad because of the monsters. She didn't intend to do it for the sake of an ordinary vagrant. Though how ordinary could he be, really?

As if in answer to her question, the man suddenly flew up into the treetops with a yell. There he hung upside down, thrashing his arms and legs wildly as he swung back and forth with his feet stuck in a tangle of branches.

Julia took hold of Edvin's arm and got ready to flee – but she didn't see any smoke monsters or any other danger. The Troubadour just hung upside down in the tree, about three metres above the ground, as if he had climbed up, fallen and become stuck.

"Boy!" he shouted. "Help me! Take the brush! I dropped it!"

"His name isn't boy," Julia said, despite the absurd situation.

"Help me, please! I can't do this! I can't." The Troubadour sounded on the verge of tears. He began babbling and whistling, and then Kasir stepped forward and searched in the dark for the dropped brush.

Julia bent down to help him. A mobile phone would have been very practical at that moment.

A sudden creaking sound made her look up. A hollow in the tree trunk was in the process of opening, widening from a narrow crack until it grew as big as her and even bigger. Meanwhile, the howling Troubadour was swinging higher and higher, getting closer and closer to the dark hole. It looked almost like an enormous mouth, intent on swallowing him.

"Help!" he cried. "Quickly!"

"Here!" said Edvin. He picked up the slender brush and handed it to Kasir.

The refugee boy whirled and pointed the brush at the tree's open mouth. Then he hesitated.

"Help him!" Julia cried. "Do what you did before!"

Kasir said something in his whistling, babbling language. It almost sounded like a question.

The Troubadour whistled and babbled back at him desperately, and then Kasir stepped forward hesitantly and began to paint on the trunk of the tree.

The tree screamed and dropped the Troubadour, who hit the ground with a thud and a groan. Julia and Edvin helped him to his feet and led him a safe distance away while Kasir slowly backed away with the brush held out between himself and the tree as a shield.

The tree screamed again, whipped its branches – and froze, becoming like a normal tree once again.

"I'm too old for this," the Troubadour groaned. "But well done, boy. Thank you."

Kasir bowed and whistled quietly in response, holding out the brush.

"You can keep it for now," said the Troubadour. "But we have to keep going. It shouldn't be too much further."

He limped on in almost the same direction as before. Julia, who took his arm and tried to support him, had to help him get his bearings again. He really smelled bad up close. And he was heavy.

"What was that?" Edvin asked as they walked. "One of those darkenwraiths?"

"I don't know," said the Troubadour. "And I don't want to know, either. I'm too old for all this. We'll just have to hope we don't meet any more like that on the way."

But what if we're surrounded by more like that? Julia thought uneasily, glancing at the tall, dark trees that surrounded them on all sides. They didn't look at all different from the one that had almost devoured the Troubadour.

Kasir walked with a nervous alertness on the Troubadour's other side, his brush ready like a little sword. Now and then Julia glanced back at Edvin who was walking behind her. He was uncharacteristically quiet, maybe too frightened to think of anything to say. She wished she could comfort him.

"Ah, here it is!" the Troubadour suddenly exclaimed after they had walked in silence for some time. He pointed to an arched shape that Julia had thought was a bent, half-fallen branch. But now as they drew closer, it looked more like an open gate made of wood.

"Come on," the Troubadour said, limping more quickly. "We'll be safe in there."

He led them through the dark wooden gate.

Edvin let out a squeak. It was as if someone had flipped a switch and turned the sun on like a ceiling lamp. Julia squinted in the unexpected daylight and saw that they were no longer in a dark forest but rather on the high edge of an enormous, bowl-shaped valley of green grass. Down in the valley, a river like a blue thread wound among cultivated fields and orchards. Among the orchards, she noticed a number of lovely stone houses with grass roofs.

A clip-clop of hooves sounded to their left.

Julia turned hastily to see a rider in white come charging toward them on a white horse. His face was hidden behind a white helmet with the visor lowered, and under his arm he held a long, white lance, which he pointed straight at them.

8

"Is he dangerous?" Edvin asked anxiously, staring wide-eyed at the white rider.

"Just keep quiet and let me do the talking," said the Troubadour. "Everything's going to be fine."

The knight came to a sudden halt uncomfortably close to them, his gleaming white lance pointed straight at the large man's chest. There he sat on his pale steed, as still as a statue. Or maybe he became a statue – Julia thought that he, his horse and his deadly lance all looked like a single piece of shiny white marble.

The Troubadour whistled and babbled in Kasir's language. He bowed his head as he spoke, and even though Julia couldn't understand the words, she got the impression that he was pleading. He sounded frightened.

When the Troubadour had finished speaking, the statue knight answered in the same incomprehensible language. As he spoke, he moved again and pointed his lance at the children, one at a time. The long, slender weapon's point was as sharp as a needle. Julia took a step back as its deadly tip passed by, a few centimetres from her chest.

"What's he saying?" she whispered.

The Troubadour didn't answer. He just whistled and babbled with new desperation.

"Julia," Edvin said anxiously. "Is he going to kill us?"

Julia patted her brother's arm. As she did this, the knight suddenly swung his lance so that its needle tip hovered between her and Edvin. They both jumped back with a squeak of terror.

"Don't move," the Troubadour hissed. He continued pleading.

Julia wished she could at least see the expression on the knight's face. If he had any face behind the marble visor.

"Kasir?" she said quietly, trying to move her mouth as little as possible.

"He not believe," the refugee boy answered as the Troubadour continued to speak. The man got down on his knees in the grass and babbled with upraised hands.

The knight answered briefly and firmly. Then he backed his marble horse up a step and drew a white marble horn from his saddlebag. Without opening his visor, he blew a long, low note that echoed over the valley.

The call was answered by three exactly like it, and presently three more marble knights came thundering towards them across the grass. The four knights surrounded them with lances lowered, ready to strike. The first one whistled something.

59

"He says we have to turn over our weapons," said the Troubadour.

Kasir look quizzically at him, and when the man whistled something quietly, he drew his paintbrush and reluctantly handed it over to one of the knights.

A white lance stabbed the air emphatically in front of Julia, and she jumped back. One of the knights whistled.

"He says that you have to turn over your weapon, too," said the Troubadour. "I strongly recommend that you do it quickly."

"I don't have a weapon," Julia said, staring in terror at the needle-sharp marble point. "Tell him – say that I'm unarmed."

It was Kasir who answered the knight, pointing to Julia as he spoke. She hoped desperately that the knights would believe him.

One of the riders whistled a short answer, and suddenly Julia felt cool marble against her collarbone. She looked down in horror at the white lance tip, trembled and did her best not to flinch. The knight had managed to get the tip of his lance under the thin metal chain that held her father's ring.

"You have to give him your necklace," said the Troubadour. "I don't know why. But take it off – quickly!"

"Will I get it back?" Julia asked, careful not to make any sudden moves as she fumbled for the clasp to the chain. No one answered her, and with deep misgivings, she was forced to turn over the necklace with a trembling hand.

When the marble knight had received the necklace and thrust it into his saddlebag, he suddenly grabbed Julia's arm and pulled.

Julia swung screaming up into the saddle behind the knight. Two of the other riders lifted Edvin and Kasir in a similar manner, and the fourth approached the Troubadour.

The heavyset vagrant was a lot larger than the marble knight – if the latter had stood on the ground, he would have been a head shorter and half as broad. Regardless, the living statue grabbed hold of the collar of the Troubadour's filthy brown coat with one hand and slung the huge man up into the saddle behind him. The Troubadour let out a cry and almost fell off, but then the knight grabbed him again and straightened him out. Then he raised his lance and galloped off down the grassy slope. The other riders followed.

The horse's back was almost as hard as marble under Julia, and the knight's armour, which she clung to in order not to fall off, was even harder. This was no comfortable ride – as the horse thundered down into the valley at a furious speed, it occurred to her that this was not at all what she had dreamed of when the girls at school had gone on and on about their horses.

The landscape that whizzed past them, on the other hand, was more beautiful than her loveliest dreams. She saw streams and ponds, fruit orchards and wildflowers, and every now and then some people in long, beautiful garments, gathering hay or trampling grapes with red feet in quaint wooden winepresses.

The unbelievable journey came to an abrupt halt at a fragrant garden surrounded by a low, mossy stone wall. Here the knight lifted Julia down with one hand. He dismounted and strode in through an opening in the wall. His marble shoes rang on the stone slabs that formed a path among the flowers and bushes.

Julia wondered if she was meant to follow him, but when she took a step forward, one of the other knights let out a warning whistle, and her path was blocked by a shining white lance.

So she stood waiting with Edvin, Kasir and the Troubadour while the three remaining knights guarded them.

"You said that he didn't believe us," Julia said quietly to Kasir. "Do they believe us now? Is everything all right, or …?"

"Everything's going to be fine," the Troubadour interrupted, a bit too quickly. Julia did not feel comforted.

After a silent eternity, the marble knight returned, escorting a short woman with bare feet and a blue dress. The dress, like the woman, was at the same time both simple and elegant, like the sky on a lovely spring day. Something about the woman's round, slightly wrinkly face and her broad, smiling mouth looked familiar, or maybe it was her curly, greying hair or her dark, cheerful eyes.

She whistled something in greeting, and her whistling sounded friendly and pretty, like birdsong by a babbling brook.

The Troubadour and Kasir got down on their knees, and after exchanging glances with each other, Julia and Edvin followed suit.

"They speak Swedish," the Troubadour mumbled. "They're from Klippsby."

The woman's mouth dropped open, and her glittering eyes grew wide. She hurried to the kneeling vagrant, took his face between her hands and looked deep into his eyes. "Lars-Petter?" she said.

The Troubadour nodded silently and lowered his gaze.

"I hardly recognise you! I thought that you … What's happened to you, my friend?"

"You don't want to know, and I don't want to tell you," he said, his voice growing strangely thick. "Just help the children. They need you."

"I'm not finished with you, Lars-Petter," the woman said firmly. "No matter what may have happened." She pressed her lips softly against his ruddy forehead, and a tear fell to the ground under his downturned face. "But I suppose I should introduce myself to my other guests," the woman continued, straightening.

She whistled a few notes, and the knights bowed and disappeared with a clip-clop of marble hooves. "I really must apologise for their behaviour," she said, giving Julia, Edvin and Kasir a motherly smile. "They

63

were created to defend, not to chit-chat – at least that's how their creator explained things. Personally, I would have given them a bit more colour, but … Anyway, welcome to my domain, Bonavita. My name is Maja Liljestrom."

Julia gaped. Now she knew where she had seen the woman's face before – in a portrait hanging in the library back home in Klippsby. Maja Liljestrom was the artist who had painted the finest paintings in the art museum, in the church and in many other places in Klippsby. She was the only artist the town was prouder of than Angelica Skogsbergh, the great sculptor.

She had also been dead for over a hundred years.

9

"That's funny!" said Edvin. "Where we come from, there's a really famous woman with the exact same name."

Maja winked. "Some names are funny like that," she said. "But what are yours?"

She whistled something to Kasir.

"He can speak Swedish," Julia said without thinking. She had said this exact same thing all too many times to the children in the playground when they tried addressing him in English – a language he did not understand a word of. Now she felt how her cheeks burned as she realised what a foolish thing it was to say in this context.

"Do you really speak Swedish?" Maja said, studying Kasir more closely. "I beg your pardon – I thought you were a Sulallian. Would you care to tell me your name, young man?"

Kasir nodded. "Sulallia home," he said. Then, after a moment's hesitation, he added, "Kasir."

Maja stared. "But surely you're not … Dear me, how could I have missed it? You have your mother's eyes!" Now it was her turn to kneel in the grass. "Your Highness!" she said, taking Kasir's hand and kissing it. "My most sincere condolences for everything that has befallen your fair domain. Words cannot express my sorrow."

"Prince Kasir?" the Troubadour said, wide-eyed. "I know you! I held you in my arms when you were …" He had just made it to his feet, but now he hastily knelt in the grass again.

Edvin also knelt. "Sorry," he said to Kasir. "I didn't know you were a prince. I mean, I didn't know you were a prince, Your Highness!"

Julia stood gaping. "This must be a dream," she said aloud. Beneath her confusion and shock, a dull anger began to smoulder. Wasn't it enough that Kasir's drawing had been in the paper? Did everyone really have to kneel before him and call him a prince?

The refugee boy whistled something and said, "Up, up!" He helped Edvin to his feet. "Up, up," he repeated, and Maja and the Troubadour also rose.

"Not down," Kasir continued. He pointed to his chest with both hands. "Not prince. Not down. Not Sulallia, not prince. Not your highest. Gone."

The Troubadour cleared his throat and looked as if he wanted to say something comforting. But whatever it was remained unsaid, and he lowered his gaze.

"Kasir," said the refugee boy. "Kasir only."

"As you wish, Kasir," Maja said with the faintest suggestion of a curtsy. All cheerfulness had vanished from her face. It was as if a large grey cloud had suddenly cast its shadow over a lovely spring day.

"That leaves the two of you, then," Maja said, turning to Julia and Edvin. "Who are you, and how can I help you?"

"I'm Edvin," said Edvin. "And if you could help me to wake up, that would be really great. I mean, it's really nice here and everything, but I'm getting tired of this nightmare, and I'd like to see my mum."

"And I'm Julia," Julia said quickly, before Maja could say the dreaded words about this not being a dream.

"They're Henrik's children, Maja," the Troubadour said softly.

Suddenly Julia found herself enfolded in a warm embrace, along with her little brother. "Is Henrik Andersson really your father?" Maja asked.

"Yes," said Edvin. "But he died years ago."

"I know, Edvin, I know," Maja said, hugging them more tightly. "You are most welcome here. If there's anything at all that I can do for you …" She looked over Edvin's head. "Come, Kasir, you're not alone here. My home is your home." And suddenly the refugee boy was also enfolded in her embrace.

Maja's embrace was like a long, warm summer day that smelled of wildflowers and grass. When it was over, Julia suddenly felt completely relaxed, and also a little tired. She yawned.

"Are you weary?" asked Maja. "Pardon me, I never asked what time of day it was back home in Klippsby. I can prepare some rooms for you, and we can talk more when you've rested."

"Their business can't wait," said the Troubadour. "There are darkenwraiths after them. And not just any darkenwraiths – I saw Korak."

Maja's expression turned grave. "Then we must speak now. But we can at least lighten our heavy conversation with some food and drink. Come."

She led them into the garden. "So you've heard of our dad?" Edvin asked, skipping after her on the flat stones of the path.

"Everyone has heard of your father," she said. "He was a rare gem among the creators."

"The creators?" Edvin said, confused.

Maja stopped short and gave the Troubadour a look. "How much do they know?" she asked.

He shrugged. "Not much, I'd guess. They can't speak the language, anyway."

"We don't know anything," Julia said, offended. "And you haven't explained any of it to us either – *Lars-Petter*. You just kidnapped us to a strange place where it's dark and then light, where the trees eat people and the statues are alive and … That statue took Dad's ring!" she realised, horrified.

"Do you mean this?" Maja said, pulling a fine metal chain from the pocket of her dress.

Julia eagerly took her necklace and fastened it around her neck. The cool feeling of the silver ring against her collarbone was a comfort.

"I thought there might be something special about it," Maja continued. "Even if I don't understand why

Roland thought it was a weapon. But this, on the other hand, I understood." She handed the dark brown paintbrush to Kasir.

"Roland?" the Troubadour said with a snort of laughter.

"Pallantu didn't give them any names," said Maja. "And I thought that Roland suited him. Don't you think so? Ah, this seems like a good place to sit down and talk."

They had arrived at a round table of cracked stone that stood sheltered on three sides by small, lovely trees. Four rough-hewn chairs of dark wood stood around the table. "Just a moment," Maja said, hurrying off to a little red cottage that looked nearly as familiar as the woman herself.

"That house looks just like a painting in the art museum," Edvin pointed out.

The Troubadour laughed aloud.

Soon afterward, Maja came back with a grey apron over her dress and an artist's crescent-shaped palette in her hand. She drew a brush from the pocket of the apron, dipped it in the splotches of colour on the palette – and painted a fifth chair, in the same style as the other four, in mid-air.

Julia gaped.

"Cool!" Edvin said, feeling the chair. It seemed to be completely solid. He sat in it. "Julia, you have to try this!"

Meanwhile, Maja was busy painting tea on the table – an old-fashioned teapot made of blue china, five teacups of the same material, a platter of bicuits and a fruit bowl. She worked unbelievably quickly, and before Julia realised she was gaping and closed her mouth, the table was set.

"How …?" said Julia.

"I've changed my mind!" said Edvin. "I don't want to wake up. This dream is great!"

Maja laughed.

"Are you … are you a ghost?" Julia asked once she could speak again.

"No, not at all," said Maja. She set the palette down on a small table she had painted for that purpose, stuck the paintbrush in a glass of water and began serving tea. "I don't believe in ghosts," she continued. "And not in magic, either, if that's your next question. But it seems I may have to explain a few things before you answer my questions. Here you are." She passed a steaming teacup to Julia. "Take care, it's hot!"

While Julia, Edvin, Kasir and the Troubadour munched on the biscuits and fruit that Maja had painted, the artist did her best to answer the questions that Edvin and Julia stammered between bites. Yes, she was the same Maja Liljestrom who had done the paintings in Klippsby. No, she wasn't dead. No, this wasn't Heaven. Yes, she was completely sure she wasn't a ghost. "I'm a creator," she said. "Just like your father. And just like Lars-Petter. And your friend Kasir."

"Creator?" said Julia. "What, like a god?" This was too much for her to take in. Wasn't it enough for Kasir to be a prince? Did he also have to be a god? "Kasir is just a refugee," she pointed out. "And a child."

Maja gave her a serious look. "And you don't think that God could show himself as a child, or as a refugee? Don't people celebrate Christmas in Klippsby anymore?"

Julia's head felt like it was spinning.

"No one is *just* a refugee," Maja continued. Her encouraging smile washed away Julia's embarrassed feeling that she had said something very foolish. "But Kasir isn't a god, and neither are we."

"Thank goodness," the Troubadour muttered.

"Crator?" the refugee boy said curiously.

Maja whistled and babbled something to him, and his eyes widened. "Not crator," he said. "Not me."

"Not yet, maybe," Maja corrected him. "Anyway, I mean that we are creators with a small 'c'. We are like small reflections of the Great Creator, but only reflections. After all, we didn't create ourselves." She chuckled. "But everyone is born with a measure of creativity – we are all little creators, every one of us."

"We can't do that!" Edvin burst out, making a sweeping gesture toward all the delicious things on the table.

"Are you sure?" said Maja.

"Well …" Edvin hesitated. "Maybe if I had some flour and sugar, and if someone taught me how to bake."

"Exactly!" Maja said, brightening. "Back home in Klippsby, you can create anything you please, as long as you do it the proper way. Here in Bonavita, just like in all of Thousandworld's domains, you can also create whatever you please. It's just that the proper way is a little bit different. And the process can go much quicker. Time works a bit differently here."

"Is that why you're still alive?" Julia managed to stammer. "In our world, you're supposed to be dead. Or vanished – my mum said so. But that was a hundred years ago, so that means you should be dead anyway. No offence," she added hastily.

Maja winked. "Time works a bit differently here," she said again. "Especially for those who have learned to use their creativity to its full potential. Here in Thousandworld, such people are called creators, and they wield great power. That's why it's called Thousandworld – they've created and created and created, and so now we have an enormous constellation of different domains. Or little worlds, if you want to think of them that way."

"Can they create whole worlds?" Julia gasped.

"Only the really talented ones," the Troubadour cut in.

"Lars-Petter." Maja gave him a look. "You underestimate yourself, as usual. You know you could do it if you would only try."

73

"No," he said hastily. "No more of that kind of thing for me."

"But do you mean that our dad could create whole worlds – I mean, domains?" Edvin asked breathlessly.

"I think so," said Maja. "Though as far as I know, he never created a domain of his own. Instead he made jewellery – very fine work, with great power. Not even Pallantu could learn his technique. But anyway …"

"But Mum said that Dad worked as a postman," Edvin interrupted.

Maja laughed. "Postman?" she said. "Maybe that's not so far from the truth. But it sounds as if your mother didn't want you to know certain things. Anyway, I think it's time we spoke about the matter at hand. What do you know about the darkenwraiths?"

"Nothing," said Julia. "We don't know anything about any of this! We just got chased away from our house by a bunch of monsters made of smoke or something, and then we were kidnapped by your friend Lars-Petter here, and we've been attacked by trees and living statues, and now you say that our dad wasn't a postman but some kind of, some kind of …"

Maja laid a comforting hand on her shoulder. "I wish I could make all of this easier for you," she said. "I really do. It must be so much to take in, all at once. But you have to be strong, like your father. I'm afraid your troubles aren't over yet."

It was almost as if the woman's touch filled Julia with new strength. She sat up straighter, determined to stop whining. *Be strong, like Dad!*

"Those smoke monsters chasing you are called darkenwraiths," said Maja. "And not much more is known about them than what you know, really. Even if Pallantu has his theories. They are powerful and dangerous, and they destroy things. Over the course of the last fifteen years, they have spread throughout Thousandworld and laid waste hundreds of domains – but worst of all is what they did to Sulallia." She shook her head. "You've all seen what's happened to my little world of Bonavita on your way here. My power is enough to protect my people in this valley – with a little help. But not to take back that which has been lost. And not to resist Korak."

"Who is Korak?" asked Julia.

"The one who was after us in the square," said the Troubadour. "I couldn't fight him. That's why we had to run."

"Strong," Kasir suddenly said. "Too much strong."

Julia remembered how Kasir had thrown a net over the tentacle monster in her living room and how the creature had just laughed and carried on. Then she remembered the larger tentacle monster she had seen on the roof as they had fled. "There was another one of the same kind at our house," she said. "But bigger."

"No doubt it was the same Korak," the Troubadour said gravely. "He's not like a human – he can be in several places at once. Well, that was Pallantu's theory, anyway."

Julia noticed that he said the name *Pallantu* with a certain displeasure.

"Korak is one of the more powerful darkenwraiths," said Maja. "And he seems to be able to control others – maybe he's some kind of leader among them, if they work that way. He was involved in the events that unfolded in Sulallia and … Well, he has caused a lot of destruction. He has also killed several creators. And if he has learned how to leave Thousandworld and show himself on Earth … Lars-Petter, we have to speak with Pallantu."

"Be my guest," the Troubadour said, rising to his feet. "Feel free to tell him. I've done my part."

"Lars-Petter!" Maja's eyes were wide with shock.

"I don't do this anymore," the Troubadour said, limping as he backed away from the table. "Never again. This was the last time – just for Henrik's sake." He turned around to leave.

"Lars-Petter Modéus!" Maja said sternly, leaping to her feet so violently that her chair was knocked over. "I don't know what's happened to you since the last time I saw you, but the man I knew would never have left Prince Kasir and Henrik Andersson's children in trouble like this! They need you!"

"They need a creator," the Troubadour grunted over his shoulder. "I'm not that man anymore. He died with Angelica. Now they need you – or maybe *Pallantu*."

Kasir whistled something.

The Troubadour whirled around violently to face him. His eyes gleamed with tears, and his ruddy face was redder than normal. "If I could help you, Your Highness, then I already would have done it! Sulallia wouldn't be a ruin! Your parents wouldn't be … Angelica would have stopped all of that, if I had just … You need someone else, I said!"

"There is no one else," said Maja. "Someone has to bring them to Pallantu, and I have to stay here to defend my people. What would Angelica tell you if she were here?"

"She's not here!" the Troubadour roared. "Don't you understand? The light of Thousandworld has been snuffed out – and it's my fault! It's too late." Having said this, he turned back around and limped away with his head hung low.

Maja seized her palette and drew her brush. For a horrible moment, Julia thought she was going to paint something really dangerous to hurt the Troubadour – but instead she quickly painted an eight-stringed instrument. Then she began to strum it, a bit clumsily, and to sing.

The song was in Kasir's language, and the melody and the voice were so beautiful that Julia desperately wished she could understand the words. The Troubadour stopped in his tracks with his back towards them.

Julia looked quizzically at Kasir, who seemed to understand what she wanted. "Light," he explained.

"Light in … black." He screwed his face up and seemed to be groping for the right word. "Hope," he said at last.

The Troubadour let out an exasperated roar and came stomping back to the table. "It's not fair," he complained. "It's not fair of you to sing her song."

"The song that one of Thousandworld's finest creators wrote for her," Maja corrected. "The man who is still in there." She thrust a finger at his chest. "The man who turned back to help just now. It's not too late, Lars-Petter. The light shines in the darkness …"

"And the darkness has not overcome it," the Troubadour finished with a sigh. He stretched out his hand. "Give me the lute. If we're going to hear that song, we might as well hear it as it was meant to be played."

10

When Julia had fallen asleep in her cosy, old-fashioned room in Maja's cottage, she dreamed of the Troubadour's – or rather, Lars-Petter's – song. In the dream, it had the same effect as when he had played it at the table in the garden. She felt transported to another place, a place that was barren and grey as a stone, where the sky was heavy with dark clouds. Then a single sunbeam burst through. The clouds scattered, Julia's heart leaped for joy, and life began to sprout up in the barren landscape – green and beautiful and at first fragile, but it grew until everything was green. *The light shines in the darkness, and the darkness has not overcome it.*

When Julia woke in the soft bed with its embroidered coverlet and saw the sunbeams slanting in through the window, she felt strong and healthy and ready for a new day. Then she realised where she was and froze with horror.

This isn't a dream, she was forced to admit to herself. *I've woken up, and I'm still here in Maja's world.* Her thoughts spun as she washed her face in a porcelain bowl that stood on the dresser. The water was cold enough to really reinforce the reality of her situation.

She got dressed. The clothes she had been wearing the previous day were gone, and now new clothes hung on a wooden chair by her bedside – some kind of short, white dress with a golden cloth belt around the waist, white trousers and dark leather shoes. It was a relief to have shoes on again, and an even greater relief that they, just like the white clothes, fit.

When was dressed, she crossed the rustic wooden floor and opened the old wooden door. Its hinges creaked.

"Good morning," said Maja. She sat at the table with Kasir, who was also dressed in white. The whole room was like something Julia had seen in a museum, but very cosy and pleasant. The furniture was old and fine, with elegantly carved legs of dark wood. The fireplace looked cheery and inviting despite the current lack of fire. Picturesque paintings hung on the walls, and colourful flowers bloomed in pots all over the room. The room was lit by the sunlight that slanted in through the many windows. Outside, Julia could see flowering bushes and butterflies.

"How are you feeling?" Maja asked, rising to her feet.

"I feel … great," said Julia. *Aside from the fact that I'm still here*, she thought. But she really did feel stronger and healthier than she had felt in a long time, as if she could run a ten-kilometre race without warming up.

"Yes, a little sleep in this valley tends to have that effect on people," Maja said, smiling. She approached

Julia and studied her from top to toe. "Paradisian clothes really suit you," she said.

"Paradisian?"

"That's how people dress in Paradisum, where you'll be going after breakfast," said Maja. "Angelica's domain – or rather, Pallantu's domain."

"Oh, right. Thanks for the clothes," Julia mumbled.

"It's the least I could do for you," said Maja. She sighed. "I really wish I could let you stay here. Or that I could go along with you. But I can't protect you from Korak, and my people can't protect themselves without me. Anyway, I'll do what I can. You'll see after breakfast. Speaking of which, would you care to help me make breakfast?"

"Umm, sure," Julia said. It felt good to have something to do – an ordinary task to focus on instead of all the thoughts chasing each other in her head.

But making breakfast turned out to be anything but ordinary. Instead of showing her to the kitchen to make porridge, Maja dressed her in a grey apron, and after painting some plates, bowls and mugs on the table in front of Kasir, she handed the brush and palette to Julia.

"I, umm, sorry?" said Julia.

Kasir laughed, and Julia shot him a dark look.

"Shall we start with some raspberries?" Maja suggested. "Do you like raspberries?"

"Yes?" Julia said, a bit hesitantly.

"Good. You can start by mixing some colours, maybe a little bit of red and white." The artist took Julia's

81

hand and helped her to mix the colours on the palette. "Perfect. Let's start with a single raspberry. That bowl should be quite suitable."

"Do I just …?"

Kasir made a painting motion in the air, and Julia sighed. She wished that the refugee boy – or rather, the refugee *prince* – would find something else to do. This was worse than when he sometimes watched her draw in art class.

"Come on, Julia," Maja said warmly. "You can do this."

Doubtfully, Julia reached out with the paintbrush and tried to paint a raspberry in the air. Nothing happened. Then she reconsidered and touched the brush's tip to the bottom of the white ceramic bowl.

A pink splotch of paint stained the white porcelain. Nothing more happened. Julia's cheeks burned. "Sorry. I'm no good at this." She looked away.

"And why should you be good at something you've never done before?" Maja asked, raising an eyebrow. "Do you think that's how art works?"

"No," said Julia. "But I'm not even good at painting normally. I'm not an artist."

"Nonsense," said Maja. "That's not what your friend Kasir says. He has seen you paint – you can't fool me." She took the paintbrush, painted the pink splotch out of existence and handed the brush back to Julia. "Try again," she said. "Paint in the air, but try to imagine that the air is like a canvas. Let the picture of the raspberry take shape in your head, and try to imagine that the air is accepting your picture as you paint. That the image is sticking there."

Julia didn't succeed on her second try, either. Or her third or fourth.

"You can!" Kasir suddenly said when she was about to try for the fifth time.

Julia turned on him, enraged. "Not everyone is a royal art god from another world!" she burst out. "Some people are just normal!"

"Every person is unique," Maja said soothingly. "And everyone can create. Some paint, some play music, some write ... This is my brush. Maybe there are other ways to create that would feel more natural for you. But come on, let's try one last time, together."

If it had been anyone else, Julia would have refused to let herself be humiliated again. But something about Maja felt so warm and kind that she gave in. She let the artist take her hand and guide it through the air over the bowl. "Relax," said Maja. "Your creativity is a gift – you don't need to force anything now. Just picture the raspberry. Receive it as a gift. Relax. Good, now let's paint it. Let's copy the raspberry you have in your mind."

The brush moved, and a small raspberry gradually took shape in the bowl. Kasir whistled with what sounded like appreciation.

"But it's her who's doing it, Kasir," said Julia. "I'm not ..."

Maja released her hand, and in a sudden panic, Julia painted the last bit of the raspberry. It wasn't completely perfect, perhaps even a bit misshapen – but it was a raspberry. Julia gaped. "Did I … Did I … No, it must have been you." She turned to Maja. "It was your power in the brush, it was …"

Maja winked. "If I have any power, I've received it as a gift," she said. "And so it is with you, too."

At that moment, a door flew open, and Edvin came rushing into the room and threw himself into Julia's arms. She barely managed to hand the paintbrush back to the artist in time. "Julia!" Edvin cried. "It's not a dream! This is for real! I woke up, but it didn't work! What will we do, Julia?"

Julia hugged her little brother and stroked his hair. "Everything will be all right, Edvin. We'll handle this one step at a time." That was something her mother was always saying, which she had actually grown tired of hearing. But it seemed to help. Edvin calmed down a bit and sniffled quietly against her shoulder.

"What's all that commotion out there?" the Troubadour thundered. The door to his bedroom flew open – and suddenly he was no longer the Troubadour.

Edvin looked up and gaped. "But he's … You're completely … You're not homeless anymore!"

The large man grimaced. His foul-smelling, ragged brown coat was gone. Now he was dressed in white, just like Julia and Kasir, but with a white cloak over his outfit. But it was more than the clothes. He looked taller, more erect, and his furrowed face looked healthier, his gaze steadier. His grey beard even looked less wild. When he took a step forward, there was no trace of a limp.

"What are you staring at?" he demanded. "Can't a man sit with his thoughts in peace? Can't he even walk into a room without everyone staring at him as if he'd grown a second head during the night?"

"You look good, Lars-Petter," said Maja. "Almost as good as you're going to look after breakfast, once you've bathed."

And sure enough, after breakfast it was time to bathe. Edvin laughed aloud when he saw the swimming costumes. His, Kasir's and the Troubadour's looked like striped pyjamas, while the ones Maja painted for herself and Julia resembled old-fashioned dresses. They were nonetheless pretty in their own way, Julia thought as they walked barefoot over the grass to the bathing place, a small waterfall in a stream that ran through a copse of trees a little distance from the cottage. The water turned out to be refreshingly cool but not too cold. Edvin had so much fun splashing water on Julia and Kasir that he seemed to forget all his fears. At first, Julia was too embarrassed to play like a child in front of Maja and the Troubadour. But then the artist snuck up behind the old vagrant and emptied a whole wooden bucket of water over his head with a laugh. Julia laughed too. Then she turned to Edvin and splashed him in the face with both hands.

Once they were well-fed, clean and dressed in white, Paradisian clothes, Maja showed them to the wagon she had packed for their journey. It was an old cart pulled by a single marble horse. The cart had large wooden wheels, a front platform where the driver could sit and drive the horse, and a flat wagon bed loaded with chests and cushions.

"But the journey to Paradisum isn't that long," Lars-Petter said when Maja showed them the clothes and tools in the various chests.

"Perhaps not," said Maja. "But it's always a good idea to be prepared, as you were always telling Henrik once upon a time. And speaking of lessons that you've taught …" She opened another chest and drew forth an eight-stringed instrument. It looked much like the one she had painted the previous day, but older and made of darker wood.

The Troubadour accepted the gift with a reverent expression and tried strumming it. "This is very fine work," he said. "You've outdone yourself, Maja."

She laughed. "I wish I could claim credit for that lute. But I didn't paint it; it was built by Quintonius."

The Troubadour gasped. "Quintonius! But Maja, you can't give this to me!" He tried to press the instrument into her hands, but she refused to accept it.

"Accept the lute for Henrik's sake, and for Sulallia's sake," she said gently. "You may need it before your journey is over."

She proceeded to draw a dagger from the same chest and presented it to Edvin with both hands, as if she were handing over a great treasure. "This is for you, Edvin," she said. "Take it."

He accepted the little weapon and, just as Julia guessed he would do, drew it out of its sheath. "Careful!" she said.

"It's beautiful," Edvin said, awestruck. And he was right. The silver dagger was simple yet elegant, with a well-formed point and a sharp edge. The blade shone in the sunlight.

"That dagger was made by a true master," said Maja. "Your father."

"Is this Dad's dagger?" Edvin asked, wide-eyed.

Maja nodded. "Warfare is also an art, though seldom beautiful. If you get attacked by a darkenwraith, this dagger can protect you. But don't be foolhardy with it. A wise warrior knows when not to fight. That was something your father taught me."

"Was Dad a warrior?" Edvin asked, confused.

"In a way," said Maja. She helped Edvin to fasten the dagger's sheath to the golden cloth belt around his waist.

Julia's entire being burned with envy. Why should Edvin get Dad's dagger? Was it because he was a boy? He was sure to trip and hurt himself with it. She thought about how he had just been crying in her arms like the child he was. Why couldn't she have the dagger instead?

As if reading Julia's thoughts, Maja turned to her. "You haven't been forgotten," she said. Then she reached into a chest and dug out a small silver hand mirror that gleamed in the sunlight. "Your father also created this. It was a present for me. But I think that you should have it. It has great power."

Julia accepted the mirror and studied it with a sinking feeling. There was no denying that it was very pretty, with its beautifully crafted handle ending in a round, purple crystal as large as the last joint of her thumb – but it didn't seem to be very practical. "What does it do?" she asked. "How do you use it?"

Maja looked at her intently. "The one who looks into the mirror sees herself," she said gravely. "If she's willing to see."

"Thanks," Julia muttered, looking down so that the woman wouldn't see the disappointment in her eyes. *So am I supposed to look at myself?* she thought. *What kind of joke is this?* Of course the mirror was beautiful, and there was something special about getting something that her father had created – but was the plan really that Edvin was supposed to slay monsters while she fixed her hair? *Maja comes from the nineteenth century*, she reminded herself. *Maybe she doesn't know any better – maybe she thinks boys should fight and girls should be pretty.* She tried to smile and look thankful, but Maja had already turned to Kasir and was busy handing him a very small glass jar full of something black.

The woman whistled and babbled ceremoniously as she gave him the little jar, and Kasir bowed and pressed it to his heart.

"So, now you have everything you need for your journey," said Maja. "May the Great Creator protect you."

11

They left Maja's valley through a gate similar to the one they had entered by. It was an intricate work of art, with curling patterns woven together in a high arch. Its golden-brown wood almost seemed to glow in the sunshine of the valley.

When the wagon had rolled through the gate, they suddenly found themselves in a vast expanse of desert at night. Large boulders formed threatening silhouettes against the dark sky, and the moon that peered out from behind the heavy cover of clouds looked sickly and yellow. There was something about the clouds' way of moving that gave Julia the creeps.

The Troubadour swore, stood and handed the reins to Julia. Completely unprepared for this, she dropped one of them and reflexively tugged at the other so as not to drop it as well.

The white marble horse made a sharp right turn, straight towards a large boulder.

"What are you doing, girl?" the Troubadour cried, almost thrown from the driver's platform by the sudden turn. He bent forward and took the rein she had dropped. When he had got the horse back on the right path, he gave the leather strap to Julia, who hesitantly accepted it.

"I can't do this!" she protested, panicked, as she struggled to keep a straight course.

"Yes you can," Lars-Petter said. He took one of the reins again. "Hold them like this." He wound it around his fingers in a particular fashion and then helped her to do the same with both. "Good. Keep a firm grip, but don't yank at them. Hold your arms like this – otherwise you'll get tired. If you need to turn, don't pull with your arms. Do this." He made a slight turning motion with his whole torso. "Great, now you're an expert. Keep it up – straight on ahead."

Julia opened her mouth to protest, but Lars-Petter had already risen and turned to Kasir and Edvin, who sat on the wagon bed among the chests.

"Give me my lute!" he said. "Quickly – we're in danger."

Julia resisted the urge to turn around and watch as the boys rummaged among the chests. She held the reins in a white-knuckled grip and looked straight ahead. So far, the horse was trotting obediently along in the right direction.

"Danger? What danger?" Edvin asked. "And why do you need the lute?"

"I'm going to play silence over us," said Lars-Petter. "But be ready, boys, in case it doesn't work. Get your dagger ready, and your paintbrush!"

And should I get my sweet little mirror ready? Julia thought bitterly. But then she realised what was wrong with the clouds.

Some of them weren't clouds at all, but enormous, winged creatures like great dragons of black smoke, gliding slowly across the night sky. She stared with her mouth agape, and her grip on the reins tightened.

"Lars-Petter," she said, indicating the sky with her chin.

"I see them," he said, seating himself beside her again. "Seekers. They're on the prowl." He began to strum on his lute, and a gentle melody floated over the wagon. "Don't worry," he continued as he played. "Just keep driving straight on ahead. Relax, let your arms down a bit so you don't tire yourself out. Yes, just like that."

"But shouldn't we be … well … quiet?" Julia asked anxiously, looking up at the enormous smoke monsters. It was uncanny how silently they glided across the sky.

"This isn't about noise," said Lars-Petter. "I'm playing silence for them. If I do it right, they won't hear us, see us or smell us – as long as they don't get too close."

"What do you mean, if you do it right?" Julia asked nervously.

"It's been a long time since I played," Lars-Petter admitted. "But don't worry. I remember. Just keep driving."

93

"It's headed right for us!" Edvin shouted behind them, and Julia jumped.

"Quiet!" she hissed, turning her head carefully so as not to yank at the reins. Her little brother was right. Another smoke dragon came flying from behind them, at least a hundred metres over their heads. It seemed to be headed straight for them.

"But how do I use the dagger?" Edvin asked.

"I don't know," said the Troubadour. "I suppose you just stick the point into things. But stay calm – if it saw us, it would be flying lower. Just let me focus on playing."

"But—"

"Safety," said Kasir. "Very safety." Then he began a quiet discussion with Edvin, perhaps to keep him calm and see that he didn't distract Lars-Petter. It seemed to work, and as the cart rolled on, the boys conversed quietly. Now and then Julia heard short whistling patches of conversation, as if Kasir were teaching her little brother his language.

She gave the boys little thought. Really, her attention was divided between the dark shapes gliding over their heads and the reins that connected her to the marble horse – and Lars-Petter's playing.

The melody that washed over Julia was something very different from what she had heard the day before. There was no mighty sunbeam, no sprouting hope or swelling joy in this song. The feeling that came to Julia as she listened was actually a bit like the night around them would have been, if it were prettier and less ominous. Soft clouds rocked stars to sleep. Sand and stones bathed peacefully in the silver moonlight. The longer she listened, the less threatening the giant seekers felt. The one who had been following them glided silently over their heads at a height of several hundred metres. It continued on ahead without reacting to them in any way.

Julia didn't react to the enormous figure either. She felt such peace …

"Don't fall asleep," said Lars-Petter, and Julia sat bolt upright. She had started nodding off.

"Sorry," she said, checking the reins and the horse. Everything was in order. *If only the horse girls could see me now*, she thought, watching the marble horse's powerful back gleaming in the moonlight.

"My fault," said Lars-Petter. "It's been a long time since I played silence – I've probably got a few notes of sleep mixed in. But you have to stay awake. Try talking or something."

"About what?" Julia asked.

"Anything at all," said Lars-Petter. "As long as you don't fall asleep."

Julia considered. What did one talk about with a dangerous vagrant as he played magical silence while crossing an otherworldly desert? "I've always wanted to have my own horse," she said at last. "No, that doesn't matter. You knew my dad. Can't you tell me something about him?"

Lars-Petter was silent for a long moment. Kasir and Edvin's low murmur of conversation ebbed out and disappeared.

"There are few good people in our world," he said at last. "And it's the same here in Thousandworld. They became one less when your dad passed away."

"Was he a warrior?" Edvin asked eagerly. "Maja said something about war, but also something about being a postman or ... was he some kind of post soldier?"

"He was the bravest man I've ever met," said Lars-Petter. "But more importantly, he was one of the best. Not the most talented violin player – but always polite. I remember his first lesson. That was how I met him, you see – I was his violin teacher at the music college."

This information came as a shock to Julia. Her mum had told her that Dad had played the violin, but the thought of the old, foul-smelling vagrant as a professor at the music college was hard to swallow. Though after their time in Bonavita he looked and smelled quite different, and he played just as well as any music professor, and ...

"You didn't answer the question," she accused.

Lars-Petter sighed. "You're very bright. Just like your dad. I remember when I corrected his first theory test ..."

"No, now you're doing it again," said Julia. "We've heard that our dad was some kind of jewelsmith wizard and–"

"Creator," Lars-Petter cut in.

"Creator," she continued, "in another world – and you want to talk about music lessons? No, you have to tell us what we really want to know."

A pained expression flashed across Lars-Petter's face, and for a moment the music faltered. "No," he said at last. "Another time. It would be too hard to tell it all and keep on playing. Let's talk about something else. You mentioned horses."

Julia heaved a great sigh. But the subject seemed to have disturbed his playing, and she didn't want the smoke dragons to find them. "I'm not going to forget this," she warned. "Some time you're going to have to tell us."

"Of course," said Lars-Petter. "Another time. Now, tell me about your horses."

Kasir and Edvin returned to their low chattering and whistling as Julia launched into a long description of her horse dreams – the dreams she had had for as long as she could remember, and which had become unbearable in year five when the other girls had started spending time at the stable and she had been left out. She went on to tell him all about the other things that her mother wouldn't let them have: mobile phones, fashionable clothes and that sort of thing. She didn't know why she was telling all these things to an old vagrant. But in a way it felt good to say them aloud.

"Angelica also grew up poor," Lars-Petter said softly.

Julia immediately got defensive. "We are not poor," she said. "We have our house, and Mum has a job and

– we're not like the refugee children. Even if we're not like Kasir, either, since he's a prince. I mean …" She felt how she was getting tangled up in her own words and finally said, "We're not poor."

"Angelica wasn't either, really," said Lars-Petter.

"But you said …"

"Of course when we grew up, she didn't have the nicest, newest clothes. But she always said that what we call rich and poor is really about your heart. She didn't have what everyone else had. But she didn't compare herself to everyone else. Have you seen her sculpture *Riches*, in the park?"

"Yes," Julia said hesitantly, picturing the two cupped hands in bronze, standing on their stone pedestal. They weren't nearly as large as the hands in the square, but they were detailed and beautiful. They tended to collect rainwater when it rained. When spring came, someone always put some flowers in them.

"Give thanks in all of life's circumstances," Lars-Petter quoted. These were the words that were engraved on the sculpture's base. "For Angelica, thankfulness was wealth. Not having a lot, but really enjoying what you have. Being grateful for it."

"But you can end up getting so left out if you don't have what everyone else has," Julia pointed out. "Like if everyone else is chatting with each other on their mobile phones all the time, and all you have is an old computer at home that always overheats and that Mum always has to use to write her e-mails …"

"Yes, a good friend is a rare treasure," the Troubadour interrupted.

Julia furrowed her brow. She wasn't talking about having *a good friend*, but about being *with*, being like everyone else, fitting in. But what did a crazy, homeless drunk know about fitting in?

They drove on in silence for a while.

"And how do you say thank you?" Edvin asked quietly behind them.

Kasir answered with a low, short note and longer, higher note, which Edvin tried to imitate.

Julia felt as if Lars-Petter's song was starting to lull her to sleep again, so she asked, "How much further is it?"

"Not much further at all," Lars-Petter replied. "I've managed to sneak some speed into the bassline without breaking the silence. And by the way, now we need to turn right, just a little bit. With your whole body now, not too hard … Perfect! Do you see that round stone with the pointy top? That's our destination. There's our portal stone."

12

The portal stone was a flower bulb, Julia realised as they approached – an enormous brown bulb with triangular leaves, which looked like it was just about to open up. The flower hidden inside would be spectacular when it bloomed.

It wasn't until they had stopped and Lars-Petter had asked her to place her hand on the bulb's grainy side that she discovered she had been fooled. It was, in fact, a stone, sculpted in an amazingly realistic manner.

"All right then," the Troubadour said when he had walked a circuit around the portal stone with Kasir's brush and painted invisible symbols on it. "Place your other hand on the horse now, and I'll do the last bit."

Julia looked doubtfully at the marble horse. It must be terribly strong, and the teeth in its white mouth were no doubt as hard as marble. But the beast accepted her touch when she carefully laid her hand on its muzzle.

Lars-Petter painted one last symbol on the portal stone, the world dissolved into black – and then the bulb burst into a thousand shining flowers.

Or at least that's how it seemed at first. Julia blinked. The dark desert was gone. Now they stood in a garden – or rather, in a city! Vines with large, bell-shaped purple flowers curled around artfully wrought lamp posts. Small bushes with yellow and blue flowers grew up between the cobblestones. The low, light brown houses were half-covered with creeping vines, and long, green grass and pink flowers grew on the roofs. The sun, which was setting behind the rooftops, cast a golden-red glow over everything.

"It's so lovely here!" Edvin said from the wagon bed. Kasir whistled something that might have been agreement.

"Really lovely," Julia agreed, struggling to take in the beauty of the garden city.

"It was Angelica who designed Bloomington," the Troubadour said quietly. "But there were many who helped that day. I sat and played for those who were creating. Your dad helped with the palace over there." He pointed over the rooftops, but then he started. "Where's the palace?" He spun around, visibly confused. "If the park is over there and …"

It was now that Julia discovered all was not well with the lovely flowers. It wasn't just that they were unkempt and grew wild all around. Many of them were brown or black, dried, shriveled. Small clouds of flies buzzed over some of these. She approached a rotten brown plant where the flies were buzzing – and jumped back with a cry.

Every single fly was a tiny smoke monster.

The Troubadour saw what she was staring at and hastily painted a light grey net with Kasir's brush and threw it over the entire bush. The smoke flies buzzed shrilly in protest, then fell silent and disappeared.

"My lute!" Lars-Petter shouted, running towards the wagon. "Give me my lute!"

He took the instrument from Kasir and gave him the paintbrush. "Be on your guard," he said and began to play. "This city has fallen. Get in the wagon, girl! We have to leave this place as quickly as possible."

Julia climbed hastily up into the driver's seat along with the Troubadour, who was now playing a rather monotonous, droning tune – something to keep the flies at bay, she hoped.

"Drive," he said. "Follow the main street." Julia looked quizzically at him. "Flick him with the reins, and he'll start moving."

She did as the Troubadour said, and the horse obeyed. Its marble hooves clip-clopped on the cobblestones, and the wagon rolled on.

"Left here," said the Troubadour. When they came out onto the broad main street he groaned loudly.

Julia followed his gaze to the right, but was immediately forced to look left as she turned the horse and the wagon. What she had seen was hardly encouraging. "Was that the palace?" she asked quietly.

The Troubadour didn't answer. He turned, staring back at the reddish brown heap of ruined stone. Some of the stones were blackened, Julia had noticed, as if marked by smoke or ash.

Julia drove on in silence. The brown stone houses and the curling blossoms lost some of their charm as the marble horse pulled the wagon onward, and the beautiful statues that stood at every crossroads looked lonesome and ominous. The city was completely abandoned, aside from the flies.

Or so Julia thought until Edvin suddenly cried out. "There! Did you see him?"

She turned so suddenly that the wagon lurched to one side, and she was forced to hastily adjust course.

"Take it easy!" the Troubadour said. He turned to Edvin. "What did you see, boy?"

"A man," Edvin replied. "Or, well – he was completely white and black, with some kind of black thing on his face. When he saw us, he disappeared around a corner. Are there any ghosts here?"

"There aren't any ghosts anywhere," the Troubadour said. "Just be ready." He turned to face front again, and the music of his lute grew faster and more intense.

The city proved to be quite large, a labyrinth of streets, alleys, dried-out fountains, overgrown gardens and abandoned stone houses. The shadows grew longer and longer, and the sun sank behind the rooftops as the Troubadour played and Julia drove.

Now and then Edvin broke the silence by trying to learn to speak Kasir's language. "It will be handy in case we get in a fight," he said. "Like a kind of code language. How do you say danger?"

Kasir whistled.

"And attack?"

Julia sighed. Leave it to her little brother to treat all of this like some kind of game. She had heard him saying the same kinds of things to his little friends at home when they played their war games. A part of her wanted to tell him to keep quiet and stay alert, but then she remembered how young he was and sighed again. If this game gave him something to do so that he felt less frightened, she may as well leave him to it.

The Troubadour told Julia to turn right towards a park, and when she had done so, she stared in amazement.

There ahead of them, in the shadow of a little tree with dark red leaves, stood a winged doe. The creature lifted its graceful neck and regarded them with dark, gleaming eyes.

"Impossible!" the Troubadour gasped. "Can it really be her? Stop the wagon!" he cried, jumping down from the driver's seat as Julia struggled with the marble horse. The large man hurried towards the deer. "Dawn!" he exclaimed with the excitement of a small boy, opening his arms wide as if to embrace the creature.

Now Julia recognised the winged deer. A similar sculpture stood in the park back home in Klippsby: *Hope*, by Angelica Skogsbergh. Julia had always liked that sculpture. In year four, she had drawn it as part of her Easter picture, and when she had been even younger, she had once climbed up on the sculpture's back and pretended she was riding through the sky. Until her mother had seen her and with some stern words had forced her to climb back down.

Now the same sculpture – or at least a similar creature – stood before her and spread its broad grey wings as it stepped forward out of the shadows and approached the Troubadour.

"Dawn, my old friend!" he said. "Don't you recognise me?"

The doe never really stepped out of the shadows. Or rather, it continued on towards the Troubadour, but the shadows followed. When the deer had emerged into the fading sunlight, Julia realised to her horror that its entire body was leaking black smoke. Dark, translucent curls of smoke danced around its graceful legs. The winged deer opened its mouth and hissed at the Troubadour.

"Dawn," the man said softly. He sounded hurt, as if he had just suffered a deep betrayal.

The beast gathered itself to pounce. "Kasir!" Julia cried.

A light grey net flew from the wagon and struck the flying doe in mid-leap. The creature fell to the ground at the Troubadour's feet, hissing and thrashing in the net. Kasir and Edvin rushed forward with the paintbrush and the dagger ready. *Right now something other than a little silver mirror would have been terrific*, Julia thought, climbing down out of the driver's seat. Her gaze fell on the lute that the Troubadour had left on his seat. She brought the instrument with her and pressed it into the man's hands.

He barely seemed to notice. His full attention was on the winged deer as it screeched and struggled on the ground by his feet. Black smoke leaked out of the animal like blood. The light grey net seemed about to burst.

"It's breaking free!" shouted Edvin, who stood with Kasir a respectful distance from the wild creature. "Troubadour, it's breaking free! Should we …?" He couldn't seem to think of a way to finish the sentence.

Lars-Petter shook himself and began to play. "I can't believe this," he muttered as the gentle melody washed over the struggling deer. "Dawn, how could this … how could you …?"

The animal stopped struggling and fell silent as the Troubadour continued to play. "We're going to help you, old friend," he said. "We'll take you to Pallantu. One of his creators must be able to fix this. We're going to help you."

The black smoke suddenly thickened, and its plumes coiled faster around the winged doe. The creature lifted its head threateningly and began kicking again. "No!" the Troubadour said, playing faster. "You can't have her! You endless darkness, you took Angelica, but you won't get her Dawn! Do you hear me?" With a roar, he quickened his tempo, playing with such furious speed that Julia could hardly make out the individual notes.

Dawn shrieked.

A string snapped, slashing a red wound on the Troubadour's hand. The winged deer pressed its front legs through the net and began to rise, struggling, to its feet. "No," the Troubadour moaned. "No …"

"Lars-Petter!" Julia warned.

Dawn threw herself, shrieking, at the Troubadour. With a roar, the man clubbed the creature across the face with the lute, which broke with a loud cracking sound. The winged deer fell to the ground.

"The dagger!" said the Troubadour. "Kill her!"

Edvin took a hesitant step forward and raised the silver dagger. "Are you really sure?" he said.

The Troubadour swore, dropped the ruined lute on the ground and took the dagger from the boy's hand. "Forgive me," he said and threw himself upon the fallen deer. Dawn began to kick again, but then he buried the silver dagger up to its hilt in her neck, and she collapsed with a deep sigh.

"Forgive me," Lars-Petter said again, burying his face in the animal's brown fur. "Forgive me."

The black smoke dissipated. Dawn whistled three notes and then fell silent. Her brown fur and her grey feathers began to darken, harden, shine – and suddenly the Troubadour was kneeling and sobbing over a bronze statue of a fallen winged deer.

The last ray of light disappeared behind the reddish brown stone wall surrounding the park. The boys shifted uncomfortably where they stood.

Julia approached the Troubadour and laid a comforting hand on his shoulder. "You did what you could," she said.

"But it wasn't enough," the man said without looking up. "It's never enough. Unless …" Suddenly he turned to Kasir. "Your paintbrush!" he said. "Give me your paintbrush!"

The boy handed his brush to the Troubadour with a low whistle. Eagerly the man took the brush and rushed to the fallen statue's side. He fell to his knees and with desperate speed began painting in the air around her.

A soft, light grey shell began to take form around the statue. "The ink!" the Troubadour suddenly said. "Give me Maja's ink – hurry!" He whistled in a way that made Julia think he was repeating the same instructions in Kasir's language.

The boy hurried to the wagon and quickly returned with the little glass jar. The Troubadour eagerly took the ink, pulled out the stopper, dipped the brush and began painting symbols on the grey shell. The shell became a hard, opaque cocoon that hid Dawn completely. "All right then," said the Troubadour. "Now we can—"

He was interrupted by a sharp whistle. Julia turned to see two black and white figures coming toward

them with determined steps. They looked like men, but completely covered in uniforms that were white on one side and black on the other, with long, white cloaks similar to the one the Troubadour wore. Their faces were hidden behind white masks with large, shiny black goggles. In their hands they held gleaming metal pipes, attached with dark hoses to large black tanks on their backs. The bell-shaped muzzles of the pipes were pointed straight at Lars-Petter.

13

The two armed figures marched straight at the Troubadour, whistling and babbling threateningly. Slowly he rose from the cocoon that held Dawn's body.

Whatever it was they said to him, he made no reply.

No, thought Julia. *It's not fair. They can't do this to him – not now, after what he's just been forced to do!*

She strode forward towards the two masked men. "No!" she said. "Leave him alone!"

One of the men turned his black gaze on her, shrugged and turned back to Lars-Petter. He whistled and babbled something that sounded like a question.

It was Kasir who answered. In the incomprehensible conversation that followed, Julia felt completely powerless. The armed men began to whistle and babble louder, more aggressively.

Finally the Troubadour spoke. Just a few short syllables and some whistled notes, but it sounded ominous. The gaze that he fixed the masked figures with made Julia think of a gathering thunderstorm.

One of the figures whistled something in reply, and both men laughed.

That was when the Troubadour struck. His power-ful arm swept through the air, and a stream of a light grey smoke flew from the paintbrush, striking the men and throwing them backwards. Julia searched desperately for some way to help, and her gaze fell on the fallen lute. Could there be some power left in it? If she could just …

The two men scrambled to their feet, aimed their weapons at the Troubadour and pressed the buttons on the tops of the barrels. Black smoke poured out, rolling in billows over the large man.

"Run!" he shouted, struggling to block the attack with Kasir's paintbrush. Light grey lines appeared between him and the black smoke, but he stumbled backwards as the two men calmly strode forward with smoke pouring out of their weapons. "Run!"

Julia took up the fallen lute and tried to play. *Sleep!* she thought desperately. But the clumsy melody that rose from the lute sounded as broken as the instru-ment, and nothing happened. She cast a quick glance at Edvin, who stood frozen in place, staring.

The black smoke overpowered the Troubadour's de-fences and forced him down to the ground. "No!" he groaned. "Not into the darkness! I don't want to go!"

Julia charged the closest man and clubbed the back of his masked head with the lute. He staggered, and black smoke shot out all over the place. Some of it twisted in the air around Julia, and now she saw faint outlines of dark wings, tails, eyes …

A swarm of light grey butterflies pushed the black smoke aside and surrounded the two men, who screamed and tried to run. But then the Troubadour hurled a long, light grey brush stroke at their feet, and they stumbled and fell to the grass. In a blink of an eye he had bound them with coils of light grey smoke.

"My lute, please," he said, standing over the struggling men.

Julia hastily handed him the broken instrument.

Though a string was missing and though the wooden body of the instrument was completely ruined, the Troubadour managed to play a melody. It wasn't a particularly pretty melody, and when he had finished playing, the two men lay motionless on the ground.

"Are they …?" Julia didn't dare to complete the sentence.

"Unconscious," said the Troubadour. "Even if they deserve worse. I should destroy their weapons too, but I don't know what would happen if they broke. They're using … How can you use the darkness?" he shouted at the fallen men. "You're men, not darkenwraiths!" He pulled the white mask off one of the men, revealing a young man's beardless face beneath. "How can you?" he said again. But both men lay motionless and silent.

"It's getting dark," Julia pointed out quietly. "Shouldn't we keep going?"

"Yes," said the Troubadour. He strode over to Dawn's cocoon. "Boys," he called. "Come help me carry!"

As if I wouldn't be strong enough to help, Julia thought, offended. She hurried after him. Together they managed to lug the heavy cocoon over to the wagon and load it into a chest.

"But why take it with us?" Edvin said when the Troubadour had locked the chest properly. "What if it comes back to life?"

"Is there any chance of that?" Julia asked.

The Troubadour shook his head sadly. "Probably not," he said. "But I owe it to her to try, at least. I owe a lot of things in this life." He sighed and walked towards the driver's seat with heavy steps.

Julia followed, took the reins and got the marble horse started. "Can the lute be fixed?" she asked after a moment's silence, mostly to avoid leaving the Troubadour alone with his thoughts.

"I'm sure Maja would be able to fix it," he said. "But not me. We need another kind of creator, with a different eye for detail."

"What about Kasir?" she said, thinking of the boy's detailed drawings. "Didn't Maja say that he's a creator, too? He has a great eye for detail!"

The Troubadour stared at Julia. Then he let out a joyless laugh and shook his head. "You really are your father's daughter," he said. "So wonderfully creative. Your dad always said that good art was about seeing possibilities. First you used a broken lute to save my life, and now … Why not? Let's try it. Kasir!" He passed the lute back towards the wagon bed. "Here comes your great test of creator talent – see if you can fix this lute."

"No," Kasir said with a note of panic in his voice. "Not crator, not crator! Too much hard!"

"Come on, Kasir," said Julia. "Don't be modest – I know you're really talented! You can at least try!"

Finally she managed to convince him to try, or maybe he just accepted the lute from the Troubadour to put an end to her nagging.

"I suppose I should thank you for saving me," the Troubadour said when he had turned back to face front. "Those weapons they were using – gaah, so horrible! Words can hardly express it. If they had won, I might have become … like Dawn." His eyes flashed. "If it was them who … No, now I should focus on getting you to Pallantu. Anyway, I owe you my life. I know I'm just an old failure and an alcoholic, but if there's ever anything I can do for you …"

Julia studied his face for as long as she dared while driving the wagon along the dark streets. "Do you really think that you're just an old failure and an alcoholic?" she said. "But you're one of those creator magicians. Maja believes in you – she said that you could create a whole world!"

"Maja believes a lot of things," the Troubadour said tersely. "Sorry, it was stupid of me to even offer something like that. I shouldn't pretend that there's anything I can do for you – I'm just the filthy drunk on the park bench and worse. All three of you will be happier once I've delivered you to Pallantu and you can be rid of me."

Julia didn't know what to say. Hearing the Troubadour speak like that felt so wrong now, as they journeyed together in another world, when he had magical powers and a steadier gaze, seemed to be in his right mind, was cleaner and better dressed. But what would she do when they returned to Klippsby? What if he became the foul-smelling drunk again? Would she stop by the park bench and greet him, while the popular girls and maybe the whole town watched and sniggered and spread rumours? Would she sit and talk with him as if they were friends?

If we even make it back to Klippsby. Oh no, Mum must have discovered that we're gone ages ago! she realised, horrified. She didn't say anything aloud – she didn't want to scare Edvin – but the uneasy thoughts chased each other in her mind, and she searched desperately for something else to think about. Then she thought of it.

"So you were friends with my dad," she said.

"Yes," said the Troubadour. "That's right."

"If you want to do something for me, then you can tell me about him," Julia said. "After all, now you don't have to focus on your playing."

The Troubadour sighed. "Julia," he said. "You don't know what you're asking. Your mum has apparently chosen not to tell you. She hasn't even taught you the language! That time when I greeted you in the park, she acted as if I were Korak himself – and maybe rightly so. She probably wanted to protect you from all of this. From me and my failures." He hung his head.

Julia remembered the occasion, the picnic on her twelfth birthday. When she had walked past the Troubadour in her new yellow dress, and he had whistled. She and her mother had acted as if it was the wolf whistle of a creepy old man.

"What did you say that day?" she asked.

"A traditional greeting in Sulallia," he said. "The light shines in the darkness."

"Do you come from Sulallia?" she asked. "Does my dad come from there?"

The Troubadour didn't answer.

"You owe me your life," Julia pointed out. "You said that you owed me a favour. This is the favour I want. Tell me about my dad! Tell me everything!"

"But your mum—"

"Can't protect me from any of this anymore," she interrupted. "The darkenwraiths are already after us. And I want to know why."

The Troubadour heaved a great sigh. "All right," he said. "I suppose I can't keep you in the dark forever." And so, as they rolled out through the city's gate and onward along the dirt road over the grassy plain beyond, he told her.

"Your dad was an ordinary kid from Klippsby, aside from the fact that he thought he could play the violin. He barely passed the entrance exam to get into the music college – on his third try. He never learned to play properly if you ask me. But he never gave up. I didn't understand why it was so important to him – except that he might have wanted to impress your mum. He mentioned something about her liking classical music once."

"Yes, she does," Edvin cut in. "In the car – when it works – she always makes us listen to that stuff."

Julia shushed him. "Let him speak! Keep going, Lars-Petter! Tell us!"

"He wanted to have extra lessons," said the Troubadour. "There was a piece that he wanted to learn how to play perfectly … Paganini. But it was far too difficult for him, too fast. Anyway, one night he came into my office when I was about to leave for Thousandworld. At that time I had three small sculptures that Angelica had created for me so I could get to her domain Paradisum, to Maja's domain Bonavita and to Sulallia. That was before … Well, anyway, your dad followed along with me by mistake, and Maja thought he had potential. She was the one who discovered his goldsmithing talents, which was a huge relief for me, since it meant I didn't have to put up with his attempts to create with his violin anymore."

"Mum always said he was a great violin player," said Edvin. He sounded a bit hurt.

The Troubadour cleared his throat. "Well, he never gave up, and that's commendable. Anyway, the jewellery he made was without equal. Your dad could do things with his creations that neither Maja nor Angelica could do. Not even Pallantu, who thinks he can learn everything, ever managed to copy his technique. And his jewellery was a huge help when the crisis with the darkenwraiths began … How long ago now? Fifteen years?"

"Did they kill him?" Julia blurted out.

The Troubadour was silent for a long moment. "I hope not," he said at last. "Seeing Korak in our world yesterday was a very unpleasant surprise. But if the darkenwraiths have been in our world for six whole years … no, I don't think they had anything to do with it. People have enough wickedness and the Earth has enough suffering of its own. Your mother has probably told you what there is to know about your dad's death. And I don't want to go into it now. You wanted to hear about his life."

"Maja said that he was a soldier," Edvin cut in. "Or a postman or something."

The Troubadour chuckled. "Yes, that we were, all three of us – your dad, Angelica and me. When Pallantu had discovered the threat that the darkenwraiths posed, the three of us travelled among Thousandworld's thousand domains. We installed portal stones, delivered messages and invited creators to join the Council that Angelica had founded. Sometimes we had to fight darkenwraiths. Your dad fought like a true hero. If there was anyone who really terrified them – anyone other than Angelica and Pallantu – it was him."

The Troubadour seemed to cheer up as he spoke about the various battles he and their dad had fought in, all the brilliant solutions Henrik Andersson had come up with to save people from the darkenwraiths. He laughed aloud when he told them about how Henrik had once managed to defeat an especially powerful darkenwraith by playing music – to distract it while Angelica struck. "A bit like what you did there in the park," the Troubadour said to Julia.

But his cheerfulness faded when Edvin asked about the most dangerous battle they had ever been in, and the Troubadour began to describe a failed attempt to save a world where the darkenwraiths had grown too powerful. "We were forced to flee through the portal stone we had installed," he said. "Your dad and I barely made it out with our lives."

"And Angelica?" Edvin asked. Julia wished intensely that she could erase his question out of the air.

The Troubadour was silent for a long moment while the wagon rolled on through the dark night. "Some creators are something special," he said at last. "That's how it was with your dad. And Angelica. But all of that – it's not my world anymore. I don't do that kind of thing anymore."

"But why not?" asked Edvin.

"No, that's enough talk for one night," the Troubadour said firmly. "It's time for us to get some sleep."

14

They had to sleep in shifts as they drove on through the night. According to the Troubadour, stopping the wagon for too long would be dangerous. He and Kasir took turns staying awake and keeping watch with the paintbrush, while Julia and Edvin took turns driving. Julia felt highly unsure about Edvin's driving. But the Troubadour insisted and taught him how to do it, and at last Julia was forced to accept that he hadn't made them crash into anything. Which wasn't really that impressive, considering the fact that they were following a straight road on level ground and there was no one else out on the road. But she insisted that Edvin should take the same shift as the Troubadour – better that he sat with an experienced driver, and better not to leave the boys alone.

So Julia shared a shift with Kasir, and as Edvin took her place in the driver's seat, she wrapped herself up in a blanket and settled down between two chests.

Kasir sat on one of these chests, studying the lute. Even though he had sat fiddling with it for quite some time, it was just as broken as before. He followed its contours with his index finger, whistling and babbling quietly to himself. But he couldn't do anything more without his paintbrush, which was with the Troubadour in the driver's seat.

"Come on, Kasir," Julia said. "You have to sleep."

The boy shook his head slightly without lifting his gaze from the damaged instrument. "Soon. First help."

"You can do a better job helping if you get some sleep first," Julia pointed out.

"Soon."

"No, Kasir, When I drive, you're going to have to hold the brush, and you're going to have to be alert. Which means that you need to sleep now. We need you. Here." She sat up, dug a blanket out of a chest and draped it over his shoulders.

To her relief, he finally agreed to go to bed. "Julia?" he said quietly after wrapping himself up and lying down among the chests.

"Yes?"

"I afraid," he said. "Not crator. Not strong. Korak strong."

Julia was quiet for a moment. "Maja called you a creator," she said at last. "She believed in you. So do I. And if we see anything dangerous, we can wake Lars-Petter right away."

Kasir whistled quietly. "You good friend Julia," he said. Then he made himself comfortable and closed his eyes.

It took some time before Julia could settle down. For one thing, the wagon bed wasn't particularly soft, and the road was a bit bumpy in places. For another thing, Edvin kept speaking quietly – though not quietly enough – with the Troubadour. But she didn't tell him off, because she didn't want to be left alone in the silent darkness with the chest that held Dawn's cocoon. The sound of the transformed animal's shrieking plagued her thoughts, and when she finally slipped in and out of sleep, it haunted her dreams as well.

In a particularly disturbing dream, she watched the lock on the chest fall off and the lid slowly open – and out stepped two men in white masks, with large black goggles. They pointed their terrible smoke weapons at her. One man's mask split in a mouth like a black, gaping hole, and he shrieked like Dawn. The other answered with a shout that sounded just like Edvin. "Behind us! Troubadour, over there! Julia, wake up! Kasir! They're here!"

Julia sat up and realised to her horror that the shouts were no dream. Her brother stood on the driver's platform, leaning over the railing towards her and gesturing with his dagger. She turned around, dizzy with sleep, to see what he was pointing at. First she only saw the road running like a grey thread over the dark fields behind them, and some black bushes that stood by the roadside far off. But … how strange, the bushes stood *in the middle of the road*. And they were moving forward.

Kasir let out a low whistle beside her. "Korak," he said.

"Sit down and take the reins, boy," the Troubadour said from the driver's seat. "We're in a hurry. Kasir! Give me the lute!"

The boy hung his head as he handed the Troubadour the instrument that he hadn't managed to repair. He whistled something.

"No, forget about it," said the Troubadour. "It was an impossible task. But take the brush, and the ink. If they catch up, you'll have to slow them down. I'll see if I can manage to get some speed out of this lute."

He sat back down and began to play – then he took a quick pause to tune the instrument before starting again. Somehow he managed to get beautiful music out of the wreck of a lute – even if the melody sounded a bit anxious.

Julia turned her gaze to the black bushes. Were they gaining on the wagon? It was hard to say at this distance.

Kasir went and seated himself on a chest at the very back of the wagon. There he sat babbling quietly to himself as he practised drawing in the air with the brush. He seemed tense and nervous.

It's so unfair, Julia thought as she watched him. *Why should he have to protect us alone, when he's just a child?* She wished that she had some magical weapon, that she could sit and keep watch beside him so they could at least be two.

Well, we can keep watch together anyway, she thought, rising to her feet. She crossed the wagon bed with unsteady steps and seated herself on the lid of the chest beside him. Together they stared out into the night, towards the shadowy darkenwraiths. Had they grown larger? Julia could make out a few tentacles. Just as Kasir had said, it was the same squid-like figure who had appeared in her living room – *Korak*.

But now there were five of him.

The Troubadour's anxious melody only made the silence worse, and Julia groped for something to say to Kasir. "It wasn't your fault," she said at last. "You didn't have enough time, and it was dark. I wouldn't be able to draw anything in the dark."

Kasir didn't answer.

"I wish I had a weapon so I could help you," Julia said after a moment.

Kasir paused in his drawing and looked at her. "Maja said," he said. "Horseman said."

It took Julia a moment to realise what he meant. *Dad's ring*. She pulled the metal chain from her pocket and studied the ring in the darkness. "Yes, that knight said this was a weapon, didn't he?" she said. "But Maja didn't know why. And shouldn't she know better than some living statue?"

Kasir whistled quietly and shrugged.

Julia opened the clasp of the necklace and put the ring on her thumb, since it was too large for her other fingers. The metal felt cool against her skin. "Maja said that my dad made magical jewellery," she said. She showed the ring to Kasir. "Have you ever seen a ring like this before? Do you think it could have some kind of power?"

Kasir studied the ring. "Not see," he said. "Not know. Try?" He held out his hand.

Julia shrugged and handed him the ring, and Kasir pulled it onto his own thumb. He waved his hand a bit, then closed his eyes and waved it again.

"Not know," he said at last and gave her back the ring.

Julia sighed. "Do you know anything about the mirror then?"

Kasir gave her a quizzical look, and she fetched the little hand mirror from the chest she had packed it in. "Do you think this could be some kind of weapon?" She understood how ridiculous the question sounded.

Unfazed, Kasir studied the mirror with a serious expression, took it, weighed it in his hands and closed his eyes. "Not know," he said at last and gave it back to her.

Julia sighed. Then she looked up and gasped. "Kasir!" she said.

Kasir turned to follow her gaze and saw the five small, flying shadows that had detached from the larger darkenwraiths. The fliers came gliding towards them at a terrifying speed. With a wordless cry, Kasir hurled several grey nets at them. The shadows danced aside easily and continued their pursuit.

"Lars-Petter!" said Julia.

"I see them!" said the Troubadour. "Let me focus! Kasir!" He whistled and babbled something to the boy.

Kasir furrowed his brow in concentration and drew in the air. A bird of light grey smoke flew from his brush and struck one of the flying darkenwraiths. The black monster shrieked and ripped the bird to pieces. Meanwhile, Kasir was already drawing a new one with his brush freshly dipped in the ink he had got from Maja.

The flying smoke monsters were now so close that Julia raised her mirror to defend herself. As if it would make any difference at all.

But now a larger, more solid bird came flying out of Kasir's brush, with long, sharp talons and a wicked-looking hooked beak. This grey bird flapped its broad wings and soared towards the darkenwraiths.

The five dark shapes zoomed straight at the bird with outstretched claws. There was a terrible struggle in the air, and the flying darkenwraiths fell behind them surprisingly quickly. The wagon was rolling along much faster than it felt! Kasir's bird jabbed its beak into one of the darkenwraiths, and it disappeared.

"Well done, Kasir!" Julia cheered.

But the boy was busy hurling a number of smaller birds at the darkenwraiths. Another monster fell to the ground and vanished – but then something horrifying happened.

A long, dark line appeared against the night sky – a black beam connecting one of the dark flyers to one of the five landbound darkenwraiths further back. As Julia watched in disbelief, the five tentacle monsters melted together into one large tentacle monster, and the flyers did likewise. When the black beam had disappeared, the three remaining flyers had become one – a horrible winged giant with huge jaws full of long, black teeth. The creature set its teeth in the giant bird's throat, and the bird disappeared. Then the beast beat its wings to catch up with the wagon. The small birds that Kasir painted didn't even seem to slow it down.

Kasir whistled, panicked.

"Lars-Petter," said Julia.

"No, boy, what are you doing?" Lars-Petter shouted, and the music stopped abruptly.

The wagon lurched to a halt, and then the flying shadow was upon them. Julia screamed and struck out with the mirror as she was thrown to the wooden floor of the wagon bed. She saw black teeth, black horns, black claws – and then only black. Something like a hard, icy wind swept over her, and she was overpowered by a sudden tiredness. The mirror fell from her limp hand, but she barely noticed.

"Leave my sister alone!" screamed a shrill voice, far, far away.

Something flashed, and then everything went black.

15

The light shines in the darkness.

Julia saw white. She blinked. The sky was completely white. No – the ceiling was white. And the walls. She tried to lift her head, but it was too heavy. She was lying on something soft. It was warm here. Despite this, she still felt a deep, gnawing cold in her bones. She shivered.

"Julia!" A figure appeared between her and the whiteness, and she tried to draw back in fear. The figure threw itself over her. "Julia!"

"Edvin?" she said weakly as her little brother embraced her. She wanted to hug him back but could not manage to lift her arms.

"Oh, Julia, you're alive! You're alive! I was so scared. They said …"

Julia couldn't keep up with the torrent of words. Too many words, too quickly. Too tired. She closed her eyes and glided back into the darkness.

Weight and warmth woke Julia from her dream. She opened her eyes and saw a figure in white with a black face press something against her forehead. One of the black and white men! She wanted to flee and managed to sit up and escape the pressure on her forehead – but then she saw the sunny smile that lit up the woman's dark brown face, and at once she felt safe. The plump, white-dressed woman pressed the small, warm cushion to her forehead again and whistled something that sounded like a question.

Julia didn't understand, but the cushion felt wonderful against her forehead. She lay back down in the bed and closed her eyes, enjoying the feeling. It was as if a flood of warmth and strength came coursing into her head and spread throughout her entire body.

The woman whistled again and babbled something.

"She's thanking the Great Creator that you're alive."

Julia opened her eyes. It was the Troubadour who had spoken. He sat in a chair at the foot of her white bed. Now he rose and stood beside the woman. "This isn't the kind of thing people usually survive – not even with Glorinda's help. She's saved your life."

"Thank you," Julia said, meeting the woman's gaze. Glorinda had full cheeks and warm, brown eyes, and her hair was covered with a white turban that matched her loose-fitting, white clothes. She looked to be slightly older than Julia's mother. When the Troubadour had translated Julia's words, the woman's smile became even sunnier, and she said something in Kasir's babbling, whistling language.

"She says that you are your father's daughter," said the Troubadour. "She sees his strength in you."

"Did she know my dad?" asked Julia.

The Troubadour nodded.

The woman babbled and whistled again. Then she pulled the wonderful, warm cushion away, stepped back, made a sign with her hands and bowed slightly. The Troubadour responded with the same gesture and a slight bow of his own. "She has other patients to attend to," he explained as the woman glided out of the room.

"But …" Julia began. But the woman was already gone.

A thousand questions buzzed in Julia's head. She sat up. "What happened?" she asked.

The Troubadour grimaced. "You were attacked by Korak," he said. "Pallantu would probably call it a third-degree attack – an emanation from one of Korak's shadows. Still potentially deadly."

The horrible memory flashed through Julia's mind. Black wings, black teeth, cold … She shuddered.

"Edvin!" she suddenly said, looking around. "And Kasir! Are they …?"

"They're fine," said the Troubadour. "Now we're all safe. I can explain everything, but you should probably take your medicine." He indicated a small white table on the other side of Julia's bed. On the table lay a white tray, and on the tray stood a white, steaming bowl.

Julia took the bowl and found that it was full of something resembling blue mashed potatoes. The Troubadour went around to the other side of the bed, picked up a little wooden utensil that looked like a square, flattened spoon and handed it to her. "Can you manage to feed yourself, or shall I feed you?"

Julia took the flat spoon from his hand and used it to dig up a little mound of the blue mash. She studied the substance suspiciously and smelled it. It smelled a bit like melted butter and cinnamon. She tasted it. Yes, butter and cinnamon, and a little bit of honey too. She took another spoonful.

While she ate, the Troubadour did his best to answer her unspoken questions.

"We're in Pallantor now, Pallantu's city. Not a particularly creative name for a creator who specialises in words, if you ask me. About as creative as the color scheme. But anyway, we're safe here. This city is the centre of the Council's power, and not even Korak can get in through its white walls."

"But where is–" Julia began with her mouth full. The blue mash was quite nice, and as she ate, she could feel herself getting stronger.

"Your brother and His Highness are at school."

"Have they gone home?" Julia was torn between relief and despair. Were they safe at home in Klippsby? Or were the darkenwraiths still after them there?

The Troubadour gave her a strange look. "They're at the Academy here in Pallantor. Pallantu's orders – I assume. The man who came to fetch them was quite insistent. Edvin seemed to be looking forward to it at least."

"Edvin? Did he want to go to school?" Julia thought about her little brother's hatred for school. The only thing he liked was playing football during breaks and talking with her when she wanted to be left in peace.

"School is different here in Pallantor," said the Troubadour. "Which you'll soon find out for yourself, I suppose. The man who fetched His Highness and your brother said that you were both to be tested."

"Tested?" said Julia. She looked up from her bowl. "By the way, could you stop calling Kasir 'His Highness'? He doesn't even like it."

"Unfortunately, he'll have to get used to it here in Pallantor. He's lived here before, and everyone knows who he is. So you're also going to have to get used to it. Who knows? Maybe they're going to start calling your brother His Highness too soon." He chuckled. "They were quite impressed when he came into the city."

"Perfect," Julia said, rolling her eyes. "As if he needed more to give him a big head. Is it because everyone knows our dad?"

"Eh, maybe partially," said the Troubadour. "But Paradisum is a domain with quite a few creators, and most of them are here in the capital city. Pallantu has gathered them here, as many as he could. But it's mostly that your brother managed to defeat Korak in battle. There aren't many who can claim that – not even among the creators."

Julia stared. "Defeated …"

"All right, defeated a shadow of Korak, anyway. It disappeared when Edvin had slain the emanation that almost killed you. But there aren't more than a handful who have even managed to defeat one of Korak's shadows. He saved your life – maybe all of our lives."

Suddenly Julia remembered the last words she had heard before everything had gone black. Edvin's shrill voice had shouted, "Leave my sister alone!" A warm, proud feeling swelled up in her heart when she thought of it. But the feeling was immediately washed away by something else – something bitter, hurt and angry that wanted to shout about how ridiculous it was. "The dagger," she said. "It was Dad's dagger, the one he got from Maja, that defeated Korak's shadow."

"That's right," said the Troubadour. "But he was the one using it."

"It could have been me using it," Julia pointed out. "If Maja had given it to me instead."

"She must have had her reasons for doing what she did," said the Troubadour. "Creators have different gifts. Mine is music, Maja's is painting, Glorinda's is healing, His High— all right, *your friend* Kasir's is also painting, but his gift doesn't work quite like Maja's. As Maja taught me once, we're all unique. *We all reflect the same Great Creator in different ways*, she was always saying."

"Reflect?" Julia said, offended. "And is the idea that you big, strong men will do that by using real weapons while I sit and look at my reflection in that worthless hand mirror like a good little helpless girl and … Where is it?" She looked around in panic. "I had it when we fought the monster. And Dad's ring!" Her thumb was bare.

The Troubadour pulled the ring from a pocket of his white cloak. "Glorinda took it off you," he said. "She said it made things difficult somehow."

Julia's hand shot out like a snake and took the ring. "And the mirror?"

"Everything else is in your room at the Academy," said the Troubadour.

Julia studied the unadorned silver ring and then pulled it back onto her thumb. "Did you say it made the healing difficult somehow?" she asked. "Does that mean it did something – something *magical*?"

The Troubadour shrugged. "No idea. Maybe she just needed to see your hands. But did you say that your dad created it? His creations sometimes had a way of … surprising one."

"It was his, anyway," said Julia. "Whether or not he created it, I don't know." She searched the pockets of her white trousers and found the chain that the ring normally hung on. "Wait a minute," she said. "Did you say my things were in my room at the Academy?"

"That's where you're to stay," said the Troubadour.

"But, but …" Julia stammered. "I'm not supposed to *stay* here – I'm just supposed to get help from that

135

Pallantu character and go back home. To Klippsby! To my mum."

The large man shifted uncomfortably. "Well, we'll have to see what Pallantu says about that. He's sent a letter to say we are to report to the Council as soon as you've woken up. Normally I wouldn't have anything against making him wait a little, but …" He coughed. "While you've been sleeping, he's already waited two days."

16

The entire city seemed to be built of white marble. The high towers, the pillars, the countless fountains and statues – even the cobblestones were white. The broad streets teemed with people. About half of them were dressed in white garments, while the others, perhaps foreigners, wore clothing of every colour and cut imaginable. The Troubadour stooped and pulled his white hood down over his eyes as they hurried through the throng, almost as if he were trying to hide.

"Wait here," he said before disappearing into a relatively small, squarish building whose marble pillars were only about five metres high.

Julia stood by one of these pillars and studied the crowds as she waited. The building's façade faced a large square. In the middle of this square, a small cluster of women and men dressed in black and white made her flinch, but they had neither masks nor smoke weapons. They seemed to be performing some kind of acrobatic dance in the centre of a large ring of spectators. Julia watched in amazement as they did flips, built human towers and turned synchronised cartwheels.

Suddenly, a little girl dressed in grey stood before her, whistling and babbling as she held out a wooden bowl full of shiny metal marbles. She looked at Julia with large, expectant eyes.

"I'm sorry," said Julia. "I don't speak your language."

The girl persisted, whistling and shaking the bowl slightly so that the marbles rolled around. She looked to be a few years younger than Edvin, maybe seven or at most eight.

Julia shot a glance over her shoulder but didn't see any sign of the Troubadour. "I don't understand." She raised her hands as if to shield herself from the bowl as the little girl thrust it towards her insistently.

When she did this, the girl's green eyes grew large with shock. Then she threw her head back and let out a piercing wail.

Julia backed away, startled, and cast a quick glance around her. People were starting to look, and a very tall man in a white cloak came striding towards them.

He said something incomprehensible, gave Julia a stern look and made an emphatic gesture with his right hand.

By this point, Julia felt ready to burst into tears. She backed away another step. "I'm sorry," she said. "I don't know what I've done wrong. I don't understand."

Lars-Petter emerged from the doorway, staggering under the weight of a large grey cocoon. Dawn's cocoon.

The man looked at him and whistled – then his eyes grew wide.

The Troubadour answered quickly in the same language before the man could say anything more. "Take two marbles," he said to Julia. "Quickly. And bow."

Julia hastily plucked two marbles from the bowl and bowed. The entire time, she was painfully aware that she didn't know whether she was supposed to bow to the girl or to the man, how deeply she was supposed to bow, whether she was supposed to bow first or take the marbles first – in short, she had no idea whether or not she was doing everything wrong and just making an even worse mess of things.

The girl smiled and curtsied in return.

"Come," said the Troubadour. He staggered off into the crowd with his burden. "Quickly."

Julia followed him as the little girl skipped away with her bowl. The tall man shouted something after them, but the Troubadour acted as if he didn't hear.

"What should I do with these marbles?" Julia asked quietly.

"Throw them away or keep them," the Troubadour said gruffly. "I don't care. But don't turn around, and keep quiet."

They trudged on through the crowd. Julia stuck the metal marbles in her pocket. After her brief encounter with the girl, the crowds and the white city around her felt overwhelmingly foreign, to the point that she felt confused and helpless. Try as she might, she could not shake the feeling that at any moment, a stranger might jump out in front of her and make an incomprehensible demand. At least the tall man eventually gave up his shouting and stopped following them.

After a while, the Troubadour paused and rested the heavy cocoon on the pedestal of a statue, breathing heavily.

"We're almost there," he said. "Just …" Then he lifted his gaze and swore.

Julia followed his gaze and saw that the white marble statue depicted a towering man dressed in a long cloak, with a prominent nose and long hair. He held a lute in his hands. She looked at the Troubadour, then at the statue. The similarity was striking. The man who the statue depicted might have been a younger, slenderer, clean-shaven relative. Or …

"Come on, let's keep going," the Troubadour grunted, lifting the cocoon again. "Hurry. We can't keep the Council waiting."

"It's you, isn't it?" Julia said, hurrying after the large man.

"Quiet!" he hissed.

"No one can understand what I'm saying anyway," she pointed out. "I don't understand a word they say. Why is there a statue of you?"

"People are fools," he answered gruffly. "In every world. Just forget about it. Ah, here we are – the Council's palace!"

They turned a corner, and Julia's jaw dropped. The palace towered over every other structure in the city, the prettiest and perhaps the largest building she could remember seeing. Graceful white bridges arched between slender spires that stretched heavenward. Beyond a moat filled with glittering water lay a garden in bloom, and beyond that, a great marble staircase.

Two black-clad guards stepped forward and blocked the way across the drawbridge with crossed spears as Julia and Lars-Petter approached the moat. But the Troubadour whistled and babbled something, and the grim-looking men drew back their spears and let them pass.

Their destination seemed to be somewhere among the palace's upper floors, judging by the unbelievable number of flights of stairs they had to climb. The Troubadour was forced to put Dawn's cocoon down and rest several times, and when they finally arrived at the great double doors that were apparently their destination, he was panting and red in the face. Julia thought he looked like he had before, when he had been a confused vagrant in Klippsby, and she didn't like the change. She wished they could take a rest and collect themselves before they went in.

But after a few seconds, the doors swung outward, and a tall woman in a floor-length white robe gestured grandly towards them and presented them in a clear, solemn voice. "Julia Andersson, daughter of Henrik Andersson, creator and councilmember. Lars-Petter Modéus, creator and …" The woman hesitated.

"Former councilmember," the Troubadour grunted, striding past her. Julia hurried after him, and the doors were shut behind them.

They found themselves in a large, white chamber with enormous windows and a long, black, horseshoe-shaped table. They stood in the open end of the horseshoe, and behind the table, in high-backed black chairs, sat about a dozen white-clad men and women with solemn expressions. The Troubadour staggered straight toward the man who sat in the middle, in the highest chair. The man was tall and looked quite majestic, with a handsome face that emanated self-confidence and power. His well-trimmed black hair was adorned with something like a white crown, and his white mantle was finer than the other councilmembers' clothes, with a curling silver pattern embroidered on its long sleeves. The Troubadour dropped the cocoon on the black table in front of the man, making the entire horseshoe shake.

The man's eyes narrowed. "Well?" he said. "Explain yourself, Lars-Petter."

"It's Dawn," the Troubadour panted. "Angelica's Dawn, Pallantu. She … She's been *changed*. They … I don't know how. Pallantu, you have to help her! I beg you! If anyone can help her, it's you!"

Pallantu raised his eyes from the cocoon to the Troubadour. "Everyone on this Council understands your sorrow, my friend, but surely you have not forgotten the kinds of questions we discuss in this room.

Life and death, Thousandworld and its thousand domains, the shadow and the light. There are plenty of craftsmen in the city."

"But none with your power. I beg you, Pallantu – for Angelica's sake."

The handsome man closed his eyes for a long moment. Then he raised his voice. "I implore you, friends," he said. "Have patience with Lars-Petter. It is obvious that he has not been himself since the … *unfortunate events* in Trikonium. But out of respect for what he once was …" He turned his gaze to the Troubadour. "Someone has killed her," he said, laying a long-fingered hand gleaming with golden rings on the rough surface of the cocoon. "Who bears the blame for this unforgiveable deed, my friend? Who has murdered Angelica's Dawn?"

The Troubadour looked away and licked his lips. "I had to do it, Pallantu …"

The handsome man's eyes widened. "No, my friend," he said. "No one played poor Dawn to death – I would feel it. Tell us what happened."

"I used Henrik's dagger," the Troubadour said quietly. His eyes were brimming with tears.

Pallantu gasped. "Surely not, Lars-Petter! How could this be? Angelica's beloved companion, murdered with a dagger that belonged to her closest friend!"

"I had no choice!" the Troubadour cried. Tears streamed down his cheeks. "They had changed her!

143

She was filled with darkness, there were men in uniforms, with horrible weapons – they sprayed black darkenwraith smoke. It was horrible. It was …"

"Necessary." Pallantu rose, his blue eyes as hard as sapphires. "And now I understand who it was who broke into Bloomington, despite the quarantine, and attacked my researchers."

The Troubadour stared at him with wide, uncomprehending eyes. "Your researchers?"

Pallantu sighed and seated himself again. "But how could you have known? You who have been gone for so many years, who have not even contacted the Council a single time. Bloomington fell to the darkenwraiths three years ago – and we have shut them in there. Now the city is a laboratory, used for developing new weapons against them. Angelica would have approved."

"Approved?" The Troubadour slammed his hands down on the black tabletop and leaned forward over the cocoon, glaring at the Council's leader.

A pair of black-clad guards armed with spears detached themselves from the wall behind Pallantu and placed themselves on either side of his chair.

"Would Angelica have approved of this?" the Troubadour roared, completely red in the face. "They used the *darkness*, Pallantu! Like darkenwraiths! *Your* researchers, you say? They're the ones who did this!" He stabbed a finger at the cocoon. "I know that it was them!"

Pallantu regarded the huge man, seemingly unmoved by his fury. "You will all have to excuse him," he said loudly. "Think of what he once was, and remember that he has not been himself. Remember that he has not been here, that he knows nothing of our plans."

"Your plans?" The Troubadour took a step back and stared wide-eyed at the assembled councilmembers. "Do you all know about this? Do you know that Pallantu's soldiers are spraying darkness like wraiths, that they're destroying what's left of Angelica's city, that they're …"

"Lars-Petter," said a very pale, bald woman with thin lips and black eyes. "Remember what Angelica fought for. Sometimes you have to make sacrifices to defeat the darkness. Bloomington was already lost – now the experiments there can help us win this war."

The Troubadour took another step back, his eyes darting from councilmember to councilmember as if searching for agreement or at least understanding. The councilmembers' faces were like stones. "Win the war by becoming darkenwraiths ourselves?" Lars-Petter said at last. "Have you seen those weapons? Do you understand what they are?"

"They understand," said Pallantu. "As you also would, if you had not left us after the tragedy that befell Angelica. We need knowledge of the darkenwraiths in order to defeat them, and Bloomington gives us that knowledge. Angelica would likely have made the same decision if she still sat in this seat."

"Don't use her name!" the Troubadour cried. "Not to try to justify this! It was you who killed Dawn, Pallantu – you and your *researchers!*"

"It was not my hand that held the dagger, Lars-Petter," Pallantu said coolly. He sighed. "And my poor, old friend, do not speak too much of guilt and death and Angelica in the same breath. I see you have tormented yourself more than enough."

The Troubadour clenched his fists and bellowed with rage. Julia jumped, and the guards lowered their spears threateningly as the Troubadour threw himself at Pallantu's table like a wild animal. But he merely seized Dawn's cocoon and fled toward the door with it. "Come, Julia!" he said.

Julia stood frozen in place.

"No," Pallantu said firmly. "Stay, Julia. You may speak with him afterwards. We need you here. Thousandworld needs you here."

Julia looked at Pallantu, then at the Troubadour who stood out in the corridor. But before she had time to react, two guards closed the door with an echoing crash, and she was trapped, shut in with the Council.

17

"You have travelled far," said Pallantu. "And you have many questions."

This was true. Julia stood staring at the various councilmembers as the questions chased each other in her mind. During the preceding exchange, she had been partially hiding behind Lars-Petter's hulking figure. Now that he was gone, she felt painfully exposed. The silence and the councilmembers' gazes weighed heavily on her, and a question left her lips, mostly to break the suffocating silence. "Why are you speaking Swedish?"

Pallantu chuckled. "Swedish?" he said. "I can speak Parrish, Igru, Karathan, and like most people in this part of Thousandworld, I can of course speak Sulallian. I can even get my point across in fifty or so minor languages. But Swedish is entirely unknown to me, aside from a few words which I learned from your father."

The pale woman who had spoken before sighed. "Explain yourself to her, Pallantu. Surely you see that she's completely confused."

The handsome man gave the woman an irritated look. "Very well." He raised his left hand, displaying a swirling blue pattern tattooed on his palm. "A collaboration with one of the city's more gifted artists," he said. "My art is words, his is images. With his power I could do this." He made a sweeping gesture, encompassing all the councilmembers.

"I don't understand."

Pallantu gave Julia a long, probing look. "No," he said at last. "There are many things you do not understand. Henrik Andersson's daughter. How curious."

Julia felt her cheeks burning, but Pallantu cleared his throat and continued. "By my power, the barrier of language is broken and strangers speaking different tongues may understand each other. Which is quite advantageous for the Council, since not everyone can speak Sulallian." He looked at a small, aging man with short, silver-grey hair. The man avoided his gaze. "Anyway, we have no time to waste discussing such parlour tricks at the moment. I know that you are being pursued by Korak."

Julia thought about the black tentacle monster and shuddered. "He showed up in my house in Klippsby. In my world," she explained. "And then we went to Maja's world and ran into some huge flying darkenwraiths out in the desert. We made it to that city with all the flowers ... Bloomington? And then ... the men who attacked us, were they really yours?" A terrifying image of white masks and large black goggles flashed through her mind.

"A regrettable mistake," Pallantu said, bowing slightly. "One that I humbly beg your pardon for. It would never have occurred to me to harm Henrik Andersson's daughter. No, the men must have become frightened and thought you were something else. There are darkenwraiths that can confound one's senses. It should not be able to work with the masks that Kareth and I have created, but …" He cast a glance at a young, blonde woman who sat particularly stiffly, with her head held high.

She cleared her throat. "The masks will be reviewed and the researchers will be given new instructions," she said.

Pallantu nodded.

Julia eyed the closed double doors. "But what about what happened to the Troub – Lars-Petter?" she asked. "What you're doing in Bloomington, is it …" The question felt too dangerous to ask.

Suddenly Pallantu looked very, very tired. "I was going to ask you the same thing about Lars-Petter," he said. "It is obvious that he is not himself. What has happened to him? Is it his sorrow over Angelica that has transformed him so?"

Julia opened her mouth to protest that the Troubadour looked much better now than he had back home in Klippsby. But she realised this might embarrass him even more. So she just nodded silently.

"It is as I suspected, then," said Pallantu. "Sorrow can do strange things to a person. I still remember the day I heard about what had happened to your father. How I wish he were here with us now! But you must understand, Julia, Lars-Petter has always been a great artist, but a very sensitive one. He was never a warrior, really – not like your father. He never understood such things as strategy, sacrifices, situations that cannot be helped. And what has happened to him – and what he has done to himself to try to cope with it – I am afraid that it has all made him even more sensitive. Has he turned to alcohol for comfort?"

"He's actually stopped drinking, I think," Julia said in an attempt to defend Lars-Petter. When the councilmembers began to whisper among themselves, she realised that this was the same thing as saying "yes", and her cheeks burned.

"Anyway," Pallantu continued, "I should have realised he would find our new weapons disturbing. Using the darkness for good is a difficult concept even for the wisest. Nevertheless, it is not those weapons that are going to win this war for us." His sapphire gaze met Julia's, and she got goosebumps.

"Pallantu, you have to tell her," said the pale woman.

"Tell me what?" Julia asked.

Pallantu hesitated. "Such a thing would be too difficult to digest in front of the entire Council, when one has just arrived in a new world and heard so many shocking things. Especially when we do not even know yet. I believe we have seen enough for the time being." His gaze swept over the other councilmembers, who nodded slowly. "Yes. Julia, you and I shall speak later, under more comfortable circumstances. But now it is time for you to see the Academy."

"The Academy?" said Julia. "The same Academy where Edvin and Kasir are? Lars-Petter said my things were there."

Pallantu nodded. "The very same. According to what I have heard, your brother is getting along well there. Both teachers and students were overjoyed to meet a child of Henrik Andersson, and naturally they were happy to see His Highness Prince Kasir again. They are sure to welcome you with open arms. Fareo will escort you." Pallantu made a sign with his right hand, and one of the guards stepped forward.

"Wait!" said Julia. "When can I go home? My mother …"

Pallantu gave her a sympathetic look. "As soon as possible, Julia. As soon as possible."

"How soon is that?"

"Time will tell. I must ask you to have patience. I understand that all of this must be very difficult. But if circumstances weigh heavily on you, remember that you have a friend in Pallantu."

"But what about Lars-Petter?" Julia asked as the guard led her towards the door.

"Do not worry about him," said Pallantu. "It would be best to leave him in peace for the time being. When the time is right, I will seek him out and see that he is looked after."

"But …" Julia began, but the double doors closed behind her, and she stood locked out in the wide marble corridor. The Troubadour was nowhere to be seen.

"All right then," she said, turning to the guard. "So you were going to show me to the Academy. Maybe you could explain a few things on the way."

The man whistled and babbled an incomprehensible reply.

18

The Academy was a strange and wonderful place. Its exterior was impressive enough, about as large as the Council's palace, but lower, broader and more squarish, without the beautiful spires or the arched bridges. But the inside was like a dream – or rather, like a series of dreams, each one stranger and more wonderful than the last. The black doors that lined the broad, white marble corridors led into the most fantastic classrooms Julia had ever seen.

One room was a cheery, warm brown chamber where white-clad students of various ages sat at twenty or so pottery wheels, making clay vases. A large, clumsy figure made of reddish brown clay stomped around inspecting their work. In another room, the students stood painting apples on canvases. Now and then, a painted apple fell out of a canvas and rolled on the straw-strewn stone floor. There were music classrooms and classrooms overflowing with the delicious smells and the hectic sounds of cooking, dancing classrooms and classrooms where the students were busy sculpting in various materials. One door led out to an enormous garden with a seemingly endless hedge maze. White-clad students were trimming hedges into exquisite animal shapes, and some of these began to move as soon as they were finished.

For Julia, the Academy would have been like a wonderful dream that she never would have wanted to wake from – if it had not been such a nightmare.

No one she met could speak Swedish. What she heard was mostly the whistling and babbling language she had come to recognise as Sulallian, Kasir's mother tongue. That and laughter. In each room, her brief visit went roughly the same way. The student who served as her escort led her straight to the teacher. After a brief, incomprehensible conversation, the teacher said something to the whole class. The students stopped working, stared at Julia and began babbling quietly to each other. Then, in front of everyone, Julia was forced to take the test.

At least she assumed it was some sort of test. For what the teacher did, sometimes with hand signals and sometimes by taking her hands and moving them, was to make her do the same sort of art as everyone else. And as she struggled with the pottery wheel or the hedge clippers or the dough or whatever it was, she felt everyone's eyes on her. The teacher's gaze weighed especially heavily on her as the man or woman (or in one case, the living clay sculpture), said something in Sulallian now and then – perhaps an evaluation of her efforts, or perhaps some instructions that she didn't understand.

Every test ended the same way: a disappointed sigh from the teacher and scattered laughter from the students. Some of the teachers told their students off and made them stop laughing. When it was all over, Julia was sent on to the next classroom, escorted by a new student guide.

After the third test, Julia looked sullenly down at the floor, avoiding the teacher's disappointed gaze. After the fourth test, she was struggling to contain the burning tears threatening to well up in her eyes. After the fifth test, she tried to tell her student escort, a dark-skinned girl who was perhaps a year older, that she didn't want to go to the next classroom. But the girl didn't understand what she said, and where else would she go, anyway? She was in a strange place in a strange city in a strange world, without a single familiar face to turn to.

There were ten tests in all, all of which she apparently failed. *I'm not good at anything*, Julia thought despondently as a young, red-haired boy led her out of the carpentry workshop. She heard a few scattered sniggers behind her, but did not turn around. She felt suddenly and intensely homesick.

Thankfully it wasn't a classroom that the boy led her to, but rather the cafeteria. Julia smelled the wonderful aroma of food in the corridor outside, and her stomach awoke and reminded her that it had been a long time since she had eaten the blue mash at the hospital. The boy led her around a corner and through a doorway, and she found herself in the Academy's enormous cafeteria.

Students of all ages sat eating and conversing at dozens of long black tables that lay spread out over the expansive checkered floor. When Julia realised this was her destination, she breathed a sigh of relief and thought how wonderful it would be to sit and eat instead of doing tests. Then the red-haired boy whistled something and disappeared out into the corridor.

Suddenly Julia realised she didn't know what she was supposed to do. Her hunger gave way to swift-growing anxiety. It was obvious that she was supposed to eat, but she couldn't see where she was supposed to get the food, and the intimidating, crowded tables held no familiar faces. For a long moment she stood in the doorway, studying the scene nervously.

A portly young man who might have been an older student or a younger teacher babbled something at her as he elbowed his way past her. She looked away and moved out of the doorway with burning cheeks. Now she didn't care about the food anymore. The only thing she wanted was somewhere to be. Somewhere where she wasn't in the way, didn't stick out, didn't get any strange looks or laughter.

But her shifting gaze found no safe haven – only an inhospitable sea of white-clad students babbling at each other in a language she didn't understand as they ate food that she didn't know how she was supposed to get. She considered leaving the cafeteria, perhaps leaving the Academy altogether – but where would she go?

No, she thought. *I'm here, and I am going to eat.* She steeled herself and followed the young man. He had just come in, and logically his next step should be to get himself some food. She followed him at a distance across the checkerboard floor and saw how he disappeared through a black door at the far side of the room. The food must be in there. She forced herself to walk with her head high, to act as if she belonged and knew what she was doing. With feigned self-confidence, she strode up to the door and opened it.

Julia hastily retreated with burning cheeks. She cast about for somewhere to hide, somewhere to be invisible. At last she stood with her back to the marble wall a small distance away, waiting for her heart to stop pounding. It was the boys' bathroom. She assumed that it was, at least, since all the white-clad students who stood washing their hands in the long marble basin were boys and young men.

But what if it wasn't the boys' bathroom? What if it was just the room where everyone washed their hands before eating? What if she was expected to do the same, and everyone was going to laugh at her and talk about how filthy and disgusting she was if she didn't do it? Julia considered going back to the room and realised to her horror that regardless of what she chose, she could end up making a catastrophic blunder without knowing it.

Finally, the portly young man emerged and trundled off towards the far side of the room. Julia made a quick decision and followed him at a distance.

The young man led her around a corner to another part of the cafeteria that she had not seen. There he got into a long queue.

At last she saw the food! A buffet table stretched almost the entire length of the room, steaming with spicy fragrances. Hungry students loaded white plates with a startling variety of exotic-looking foods. Julia followed the young man's example and took a plate, as well as a flat spoon and a two-pronged fork, from a counter by the wall. Then she stood in line behind him.

Now she felt that she could finally breathe a sigh of relief. She had found the food, and soon she would be eating. The wonderful smells tickled her stomach, and her hunger awoke again as the queue crept forward toward the buffet table.

Finally it was time for her to help herself to the bounty of the buffet. She did not recognise a single dish, but she loaded her plate with something like yellow rice, a small heap of roasted vegetables and something resembling small, greenish black sausages. Everything smelled heavenly. At the far end of the table were a number of sauces of various colors and consistencies, and she took a dollop of a creamy, white sauce.

The young man in front of her babbled and whistled cheerfully as he approached a white-haired, wrinkled woman who stood in a little window just past the buffet table. They exchanged a few words, and the young man pulled out a small wooden tag that he had on a thread around his neck. The woman examined it, wrote something in a large book and waved him on. Then her gaze fell on Julia and her heaping, steaming plate.

The woman said something in Sulallian and cocked her head to one side.

"I don't understand," Julia said, panicked. "I can't speak your language."

The woman's eyes widened, then they narrowed. She stabbed a finger at the book, then at Julia.

"I'm sorry," said Julia. "But I don't know what you mean." She could hear her voice growing shrill with panic.

The woman's tone became sharper, and she gestured emphatically at the book. Julia suddenly became aware of the sound of muttering behind her. The other students were growing impatient. She heard some sniggers and considered abandoning her plate and walking away.

But then a dark-haired boy approached with hurried steps and whistled a few short notes at the old woman. Kasir! Julia had never felt so glad to see him. The refugee boy – or rather, the prince – indicated Julia with a wave of his hand as he babbled in a gentle yet firm manner.

The old woman bowed deeply and answered incomprehensibly.

Kasir turned to Julia. "Come," he said. "Good now. All good. Not cry. Come."

Julia realised that her eyes were brimming with tears. *But I'm not really crying*, she thought, offended, wiping her eyes as she followed her friend.

"What did I do wrong?" she asked as they crossed the room together.

"Not wrong," said Kasir. "Not wrong. You need …" He pulled out a little red tag that hung on a thread around his neck. "But you get, you get! Later."

All of this was almost more than Julia could bear – seeing a friendly face, getting help, hearing her mother tongue … She wiped her eyes again. "Thank you, Kasir," she said quietly.

The boy smiled broadly. "Not thank you," he said. "You do same."

Julia thought back to Kasir's first time in the cafeteria back home in Klippsby. "Julia, you're kind," the teacher had said, dropping the responsibility for the new boy firmly onto her shoulders. "Can't you take care of our new friend here and see to it that he gets some food?" Julia remembered the frustration she had felt over the fact that the horse girls were going to see her sitting with the strange new boy. As if she wasn't enough of an outsider already.

Now the memory made her queasy with guilt.

Kasir didn't seem to notice. He was quite cheerful as he led Julia to a table where she got to see another familiar face. "Edvin!" she said. The sight of her little brother made her so warm inside that her guilty feelings evaporated, along with the lingering humiliation of the failed tests. Edvin sat among a group of boys who were eating and chatting happily with each other. At once their conversation fell silent, and the boys' eyes turned to her.

"Julia!" Edvin said, smiling broadly. He stood up and embraced her, almost making her drop her plate. "You're awake! You're here! Are you all right?"

"Yes, I'm fine, I'm fine," Julia said, moved by his enthusiasm. "Were you so worried?"

"I thought you were … They said … Oh, Julia, I'm so happy to see you!" He hugged her again.

Julia never wanted to let her little brother go. But then she became aware of all the eyes on them, and she pulled out of the embrace.

Now Kasir took over and began a round of introductions. He said something incomprehensible to the boys, pointed to her and said, "Julia."

The boys repeated her name with varying degrees of success. Then, one after another, they laid their right hands on their left shoulders, nodded at Julia and said something she assumed was their names. She didn't know if she was expected to repeat the names as they had done with hers. Some of them were so difficult that she didn't even dare to try. At least she got to learn that an older boy with dark brown skin and black, curly hair was named "Hullevin".

When the introductions were over, Kasir said, "I go get," and disappeared. Hullevin indicated an empty seat beside his, across from Edvin, and Julia went around the table and seated herself.

Hullevin said something in Sulallian.

"He says welcome," Edvin explained.

Julia stared at her little brother. "How do you know that?"

He shrugged. "His Highness taught me a little," he said. "And my new friends have taught me even more." He nodded towards the boys.

"Can't you just call him Kasir?" Julia said. At once she felt everyone's gazes on her.

"It would probably be better not to say his name aloud," Edvin said quietly. "Only the teachers use his name, and only with a special title. But maybe you want to thank Hullevin. You can say this." He whistled a short, low tone, followed by a long, high tone.

Julia turned towards the older boy, forced herself to smile, and copied her little brother's whistling.

Hullevin's eyes widened. Then he laughed good-naturedly, and the rest of the boys laughed along with him.

Julia turned to her brother, a bit crushed by her failure. "Did I say something wrong?" she asked.

Edvin's brow furrowed. Then he whistled something to the short, blonde boy beside him.

The boy babbled something in reply. Then, when he saw Edvin's blank expression, he said something else, very slowly, and raised his fists.

163

"Oh, I get it." Edvin laughed. "What you said sounds a little bit like something we say in our lessons. It means that you want to fight Hullevin."

Julia turned in horror to the large older boy, but he just gave her a sunny smile and patted her on the back as he babbled and whistled.

"What did he say?" she asked.

Edvin shrugged. "I don't know. But he's kind. He probably thinks it's funny, like a joke."

Julia tried to do something to show the older boy her appreciation and to apologise, hopefully without making the situation worse. The result was a weak smile and a slight nod that she hoped didn't mean anything bad. Then she turned her attention to her food.

The boys returned to their cheerful conversation while she tasted one of the greenish black sausages. It seemed to be meat, and it was greasy and spicy and delicious. She followed it with some rice that tasted a bit sweeter than she had expected.

"Have you seen the Troubadour?" asked Edvin.

"Yes, I have," said Julia. "But I don't know where he is now. It's a long story." She didn't want to talk about the man's humiliation here in front of everyone, even if the others wouldn't understand what she said. "By the way, did you say that you had had a lesson? Have you also had to do a bunch of crazy tests?"

"Tests?" said Edvin. "No, I just train. It's fun." He shovelled some kind of stew into his mouth.

"Fun?" Julia said, thinking of the day's endless series of humiliations. "What kind of training are you doing?"

"I'm learning to fight," Edvin said proudly with his mouth full of food. Julia resisted the urge to tell him off in front of his friends. "The Troubadour said that when the teacher heard about what had happened on the road, he wanted me to join the class. Which was lucky, because I think all the other classes do a bunch of boring art stuff. You'd probably love it." He grimaced. "But it's really fun to learn how to fight, and everyone says I'm good at it. Maybe because no one else has defeated Korak." He swelled up with pride.

A small part of Julia thought she should thank her little brother for saving her life. But now, seeing his self-confident smile and hearing about how easily things had gone for him, she felt a deep, burning frustration. "It was only a part of Korak, not the whole thing," she pointed out. "And it was Dad's dagger that defeated him. Anyone could have used it and done the same thing."

Seeing Edvin's smile disappear gave Julia a terrible satisfaction, which in turn made her feel a tiny bit ashamed. But not enough to apologise.

She went back to her eating, and Edvin disappeared into the boys' conversation. *As if he can really understand anything they're saying*, Julia thought as she ate in silence. *Ridiculous.*

But now and then, Edvin whistled or babbled something. Sometimes his tries provoked a little laughter and sometimes one of the boys corrected his pronunciation, but he laughed along with them, tried again and seemed quite happy. After a while one of the boys brought out a bunch of small, white porcelain tiles with little swirling symbols on one side, and Edvin became completely engrossed in whatever it was they started playing.

Julia suddenly realised how thirsty she was. She saw that Edvin had a black mug full of something that looked like juice, but she didn't want to ask him where he had got it. Right now she didn't want his help with anything.

Fortunately, Kasir brought a mug for her when he finally returned. And he gave her a little red tag on a thread, which she hung around her neck.

19

After dinner, Julia was subjected to more humiliating tests. Now, having spoken with Kasir on the subject, she at least understood what they were all about. Every student in the school had some special gift for creating. The course of studies started the same way for everyone: try everything and find out what you're good at. The only problem was that Julia didn't seem to be good at anything. The weaving teacher was just as disappointed by her poor performance at the loom as the teacher in the smithy and the calligraphy teacher. After these failures, it was time for her to try her hand at martial arts.

The classroom was an enormous gymnasium with a wooden floor, and the students there were busy practising all kinds of armed and unarmed combat in small groups. A long row of students were kicking and punching the air in time with each other while a teacher whistled instructions. Another group were practising slow, flowing movements with long wooden staffs. Some stood beating up punching bags while others wrestled on grey mats.

Edvin stood in a corner, throwing knives at a target with some of his friends from the dinner table. Julia was quite satisfied to see one of his knives bounce off the target and fall to the floor with a clatter. But he didn't seem particularly concerned – he just picked up the knife and tried again.

Julia didn't have much time to celebrate his failure. The young woman who had escorted her from the calligraphy classroom presented her to one of the teachers, a short, bronze-skinned man in a loose-fitting black outfit. After a very short explanation from the young woman, the teacher brightened and spoke a few eager words in Sulallian. Then he took Julia by the hand and led her to the target where her brother was throwing his knives.

The teacher raised his voice and addressed the entire class, and students all over the room ceased their training and came hurrying to gather around them. A few older students ran off and returned with something large and black that they placed on the floor a small distance away. Julia turned her head to see what it was – and jumped back with a shriek.

A darkenwraith stood before her, black and terrible, with dark curls of smoke rising from its tentacles.

No one else in the room seemed to react to the monster. Except that they laughed.

Julia looked around in confusion as she took another step back. Then she realised the darkenwraith stood on sprawling wooden legs like the base of a coat rack, and it was completely motionless, aside from the smoke rising from it.

"It's all right, Julia," Edvin said, appearing beside her. "I got scared too, the first time I saw it."

"Is it … dead?" Julia asked hesitantly, studying the motionless darkenwraith.

"I don't think it's even real," said Edvin. "If I've understood properly, someone's *created* it – you know, like Maja did with the chair and everything."

"But, why …?" said Julia. But now, when she understood that the dark figure wasn't dangerous, it dawned on her that everyone was laughing at her. Her cheeks burned, and she felt sorely tempted to leave the room.

The short teacher said something to her and held out a knife with the handle towards her.

"He wants you to stab it," Edvin explained. "I had to do the same thing, maybe to show how strong I am. It's supposed to change colour."

Julia took the knife. It was heavier than it looked, and not especially sharp. "How did it go for you?" she asked.

"It went great!" Edvin said, brightening. "It changed colour all the way to blue. Everyone seemed really impressed."

Julia sighed and took a step closer to the horrible mannequin. It looked unsettlingly real. "So what's the trick?" she said. "Am I just supposed to stab it as hard as I can?" She heard the note of hope in her own voice. If Edvin had succeeded at this, then it should be a breeze for her. After all, she was stronger than him – or at least, she had been last year. It had been a while since they'd wrestled.

Edvin shook his head. "No, I think it's about so-mething else," he said. "You're supposed to stab it *just right*, or *feel* it the right way. I think. When I tried, it felt like I became a part of the dagger or it beca-me part of me or something like that. I can't really explain it."

Julia gave him a look. "You used Dad's dagger, didn't you?"

Edvin shifted uncomfortably. "Well, yes," he said. "But …"

Julia held out her hand. Behind her, the teacher cle-ared his throat, but she ignored him.

With a sigh, Edvin gave her the dagger. She laid the other knife on the floor, which got a gasp from the crowd. But her humiliation already felt complete, so she couldn't be bothered about whatever shocking mistake she had made. Now it was time to show eve-ryone that she was actually good at something. Or at least it was time to cheat like Edvin and show everyo-ne that her father's dagger was good at something. She took another step toward the darkenwraith mannequ-in, took a deep breath and then thrust the dagger into it with all her might.

The blade slipped easily into the dummy's rubbery black abdomen – and nothing happened. The class began to mutter. Julia heard a laugh.

"Didn't you say it was supposed to change colour?" she said, taking a step back. The dagger remained, stuck in the false darkenwraith.

"Yes," said Edvin. "Wait, I'll show you." He stepped forward and took the dagger.

"No," Julia said sternly, and a sudden, overpowering torrent of rage filled her voice, as if the word erupted from her mouth like a cascade of lava from a volcano. "No, Edvin – don't try to humiliate me in front of everyone. You know that I'm stronger than you. Don't try to prove that you're better than me – you're not!"

Edvin's eyes widened in shock, then they narrowed. Without saying a word or taking his eyes off Julia, he thrust the dagger into the false dummy.

The false darkenwraith remained black.

A murmur went through the crowd. Edvin stared in disbelief at the dagger, then at the mannequin. He pulled the blade out and stuck it in again, to no avail. "Something's wrong," he said.

Julia laughed derisively, and the crowd of students laughed with her. She rode triumphantly on the mighty wave of laughter. She wasn't the one being humiliated this time. Now she was the one laughing, she was the one on top.

Edvin looked completely devastated as he continued sticking the dagger into the dummy fruitlessly. "There must be something wrong with it," he said. He turned to the teacher.

The short man strode forward and looked first at Edvin, then at the mannequin, then at Julia. Something in his eyes made her stop laughing and blush. Maybe

Edvin had had enough now. The sight of the tears welling up in his eyes made her look away.

The teacher whistled, and a tall, bronze-skinned girl with black hair in three braids stepped forward and took the dagger from Edvin's hand. With a contemptuous smile, she thrust it into the false darkenwraith. Immediately it changed colour to grey, then to green, then blue, then finally, purple.

A part of Julia wanted to cheer along with the rest of the students. This had to be better than Edvin's first go that he had been so proud of – and it was a girl who had beaten him! If Maja had seen this, maybe she would have given the dagger to Julia, and Edvin would have had to play with the pretty little mirror instead!

Then the girl pulled the dagger out of the dummy, made an exaggerated bow to Edvin and held the dagger out with the handle towards him.

With burning cheeks, he nodded and reached out his hand to accept the weapon – but then, with a flick of the tall girl's wrist, the dagger flew spinning up into the air. She caught it in her other hand and held it over Edvin's head, too high for him to reach.

Julia saw red. *Dad's dagger!* Without even realising what she was doing, she suddenly stood between the girl and her little brother, glaring into the girl's light brown eyes. "Give him back the dagger!" she roared. "It's his! Not yours!"

The girl stared at her in confusion, and it was then that Julia realised what she was doing. The girl was taller than her, larger, older, and clearly an expert in fighting – that was her art, after all.

The teacher whistled sharply, and the tall girl turned to him, bowed and then gave the dagger back to Edvin. The teacher picked up the knife that Julia had laid on the floor and said something that she didn't understand. She understood the tone, however – she had failed once again.

The last test of the day was also a failure. In fact, it was the most painful failure of all, because it was drawing, the only art Julia had thought that she was any good at. And Kasir, who had once appeared at her school and taken her place as the class artist, was there to witness her humiliation.

Julia didn't want to look anyone in the eye afterward. She barely noticed Kasir exchanging a few Sulallian words with the teacher. She just wished someone would take her away from this awful place. It was Kasir who was assigned to finally escort her to her next destination. He smiled as they left the classroom together, and she hated him for it.

"Not cry," he said once they were alone out in the corridor. "Not cry."

"I'm not crying," Julia insisted. "I'm angry."

"Drawing," he said. "Good sometimes, bad sometimes."

Julia snorted. "Yes, sometimes you're a prince and an art god from another world, with magical powers and an infuriating smile. And sometimes you're just a stupid girl from Klippsby who fails at a hundred different tests and isn't good at anything."

"No, no," said Kasir. "Not fail! Not!"

"Don't you understand, Kasir? Some people fail sometimes."

Kasir babbled something and screwed his face up in a pained expression. "Julia," he said. "Not understand. Not can speak. Not. Are not … You … I …" He let out a guttural sound of frustration and led her on in silence.

Julia walked in her own dark thoughts, hardly noticing where Kasir led her. They climbed more than one staircase, and soon they found themselves in a narrower corridor, where the doors were white instead of black and stood closer together.

"Everyone here," Kasir said, gesturing towards the doors. "Not you."

Julia gave him a confused look and tried to decide whether this was some sort of insult. When was he going to learn to speak proper Swedish? But then she thought about how she had tried to thank Edvin's friend Hullevin in the cafeteria and realised how absurd the thought was.

"Not Edvin," Kasir continued. "Not me. Everyone … *other*. Come." He led her onward, around a corner, up another flight of steps and down a new corridor. The doors here were further apart and made of something that looked like silver.

"Me," Kasir said, opening one of the doors.

On the other side of the door was a bedroom that truly suited a prince, with thick, wine-red mats on the marble floor, beautiful furniture of dark, expensive-looking wood, an enormous bed that made Julia realise how tired she was, and a huge window with an incredible view of the city.

"So all of this is your room?" Julia said. "Do you really have to show it off and brag about how nice it is? Can't you just show me to the next classroom and get this over with?"

Kasir sighed in frustration. "Not classroom," he said. "Finish. Come." He led her to the next door. "Edvin," he said, pointing. They proceeded to the next door. "Julia." He opened the door and showed her a room that was almost as large and luxurious as his own.

Julia gaped. "My … my room?" she said, looking around in wonder.

Kasir whistled. "Yes."

Julia stepped over the threshold, took off her shoes and felt the thick, dark blue mat through her socks. Her eyes swept across the room, taking in the beautiful paintings that hung on the walls, the white marble buildings tinged pink with sunset outside the great window. This room was nearly as large as her entire house back home in Klippsby. She had never lived in so much luxury. Imagine if the horse girls could see her now!

She discovered a door leading into a bathroom of her own, with a large, round bathtub sunk into the marble floor. A fine white bathrobe hung among the towels on the wall. *No worn-out pony pyjamas here!* Right now she wanted nothing more than to sit in a hot bath and then stretch out on the soft, spacious bed.

But Kasir took her hand and pulled her gently towards the door.

Julia yanked her hand away. "You can't just pull on me like that!" she said, tired of everyone doing exactly that all day.

"Come," said Kasir. "More. More yours. Come!"

With a reluctant sigh, Julia followed him back out into the corridor and down another staircase.

Soon they had arrived in cavernous room with an expansive wooden floor dotted with desks. These were no small school desks like the ones Julia was used to, but rather large, proper desks with real drawers and spacious tabletops. Most of them were covered with various odds and ends: drawings, tools, half-finished clay sculptures, small canvases on little easels. The room was largely empty of people, aside from a few older students who sat working on various art projects.

Kasir led Julia towards the enormous window, where an older boy sat drawing in a large sketchbook. He was working on a picture of a girl in a long dress, with a flower in her hand. Julia studied the boy's high cheekbones and his serious green eyes. Something in her wished fervently that she were that girl.

Kasir whistled and babbled something, and the boy stopped drawing at once and rose to his feet. He whistled and bowed deeply. Then Kasir gestured toward Julia and said something unintelligible. The boy placed his right hand on his left shoulder and bowed with a smile that made her heart beat strangely. "Doneus," he said.

"Hi, Doneus," Julia said clumsily. "I mean …" Right, he couldn't understand her. She placed her own right hand on her left shoulder and bowed. "My name is Julia."

"Mynamus Jolia," the boy repeated hesitantly.

Julia giggled. "No, no," she said. "Just Julia – Julia." Doneus gave her a confused smile.

Then Kasir said something in Sulallian, and Doneus bowed again and began to pack up his things.

"Me," Kasir said, pointing the next desk over. His desk was a mess. Piles of unfinished but beautiful drawings lay among paintings, half-formed clay figures, various tools and lots and lots of pens, pencils and brushes. On top of a pile of sketchbooks lay the Troubadour's lute, still broken.

Julia picked it up and studied the hole. She plucked absently at a string and wondered where the Troubadour was at the moment.

"No," said Kasir. "Not good." He took the lute from her and placed it on the desk. "Not good," he said again. He seemed ashamed.

Doneus returned to his desk and picked up a pile of sketchbooks and a small vase full of pens. Julia watched as he carried these things away to another desk in a different part of the room.

"What's he doing?" she asked, confused.

Kasir pointed to the desk which the older student was busy emptying. "You," he said.

"Kasir!" Julia said, shocked. "You can't just tell him to move to another desk like that! If you think you need to feel bad for me, you're wrong! I can sit anywhere, with anyone! You can't just …"

Kasir shook his head vehemently. "No, no! Not me, not me. Teacher."

Julia looked at him, uncomprehending. "So the teacher said that Doneus was supposed to move?"

"That you. Teacher said that you. Here."

"The teacher said I was supposed to sit here, beside you? Which teacher? The woman in that last classroom? But I failed the test!"

Kasir's face lit up. "Yes! No! No! Not failed. Drawing hard. Sometimes good, sometimes bad. I say teacher you good."

Julia tried to puzzle out what Kasir meant. "So you told her that I'm good at drawing?" she said. "And I didn't fail?"

"Little fail," Kasir admitted a bit reluctantly.

"So I'm in the class?"

"Little in. Teacher say I help. I teach you. You test again."

Julia stared. "You … are going to teach me?"

Kasir nodded eagerly. "Understand! You understand!"

Now Doneus had finished emptying his desk. With a broad smile, he made a sweeping gesture towards the chair. Julia blushed, and her embarrassment gradually boiled up to rage. How could Kasir embarrass her in front of Doneus like this? And how could the teacher make him her tutor? The day's many humiliations piled up inside her and caught fire, and she whirled around and confronted Kasir, eyes blazing.

"So *you* are supposed to teach *me*? You think you're so talented with your god-like creator powers that you can just take me when I haven't succeeded with anything and teach me better than the real teachers can? Do you think you can fix me, *Your Highness*?"

Kasir gaped. "I … not …"

"No, Your Highness, maybe it's time that I teach you something. You can't do everything. You think you're so good at everything, but there are some things you just can't fix. Sometimes even you fail!" Julia picked up the broken lute and dropped it in the waste basket next to Kasir's desk. Then she turned on her heel and stormed out of the room, toward her bedroom.

When Julia arrived in her room, she discovered that two of the chests Maja had sent with them stood next to her bed. In one of the chests, she found the hand mirror, and having nothing better to do, she took it out. She perched on the edge of the bed, weighing the mirror in her hands and studying it.

It really was quite beautiful. With its glittering purple jewel, it was without a doubt the prettiest and most valuable thing she owned. And more importantly, it had been made by her father.

As Julia played with the mirror, her eye was caught by her own reflection. Almost reluctantly she turned the mirror all the way towards herself and gazed into it. What she saw was not particularly encouraging. Her brown, wavy hair was completely wild. Had she really stood before the Council and every single teacher and student in the whole Academy – and Doneus – with her hair like that? It was also apparent that she had been crying.

The longer she looked, the worse it got. It was as if she saw the hard look she had given Kasir as she had thrown the lute into the waste basket. In the corners of her mouth, she almost saw the derisive laugh she had unleashed on her little brother when he had failed.

I'm horrible, she thought, and almost as if she wanted to punish herself, she looked even deeper into the mirror. She looked for the girl who had failed every test, who had made a fool of herself in front of everyone, who had proven that she didn't have any talent at all.

But try as she might, she couldn't find that girl. Instead, the mirror showed her a girl who was afraid, who was in a strange world, who had struggled. Maja's words echoed in her head: *We are like small reflections of the Great Creator.* Julia didn't really understand what the words meant or why they came to her now, but when they had faded, they left a warmth behind, a feeling of being loved. Almost as if the mirror wanted to say that it was a gift from her dad, that he had loved her, that he would have been proud of her.

Tears streamed down Julia's cheeks as she let the mirror fall to the bed, and at once she understood two things. First, this mirror was more than just some pretty trinket. Second, she had to find Edvin and Kasir and apologise to them.

20

Julia's first night at the Academy was a restless one, with much tossing and turning and little sleep. At least she felt a tiny bit of peace when she thought about how she had asked Kasir and Edvin for forgiveness, and perhaps it was that peace that finally silenced her anxious thoughts and allowed her to drift off to sleep.

Nevertheless, she was not looking forward to her lessons when she woke up the next morning. After all, she was expected to go to a class where everyone had already seen her fail the test, where she couldn't speak the language – and where *Kasir* was going to be her tutor!

But first, she was apparently supposed to eat breakfast. After bathing and drying and brushing her hair as well as she could, she heard a knock at her door. She opened and saw Edvin and Kasir, who were laughing together about something. They led her down to the cafeteria. This time, with her little red tag, she was able to get her food without incident. Breakfast was as nice as dinner had been the day before. And with a little help from Edvin and Kasir, she even managed to greet the boys at the breakfast table. Hullevin seemed impressed.

Julia got no more than halfway through her breakfast before a sudden silence fell over the room. She followed the boys' gazes and saw a towering man in a black and white uniform come striding over the checkerboard floor. He held a poleaxe in one hand, and he was headed straight for her.

The man stopped at her table, looked at her and said something in a deep, booming voice.

Before Julia could react, Kasir answered briefly and quite sternly. She couldn't understand his words, but the tone was one she had never before heard from him. Now he was a prince speaking to a subject – an angry prince. He glared at the hulking man, his dark brown eyes as hard as stones. The man stared back at him, unmoved. Julia felt a dangerous tension in the air.

At last the huge man nodded and whistled a few low notes, and it was almost as if everyone at the table – or perhaps everyone in the whole cafeteria – breathed a collective sigh of relief.

Kasir turned to Julia. "He take you," he said. "*After* eat. You eat. He wait."

"But …" Julia looked at the man's wicked-looking poleaxe. With it, he could probably cut her in half with a single stroke. "But why does he want to take me? And where? What does he want?"

"Pallantu," said Kasir. "Pallantu say."

Julia rose to her feet. Did Pallantu want to speak with her? Was he ready to say when she was going to get to go home?

Kasir motioned for her to sit again. "Eat, eat," he said. "Important eat. Pallantu wait."

It was the most uncomfortable meal Julia had ever eaten. The cafeteria remained deathly silent as she gobbled down the last of her breakfast in great haste, with trembling hands. Pallantu's messenger remained where he stood, directly behind her. The shadow of his poleaxe fell over her plate.

The huge guard did not escort Julia to the Council's palace as she had expected. Instead, their destination turned out to be a graceful white tower in the centre of a sprawling garden surrounded by an imposing marble wall. Not a soul was to be seen in the garden, and no birds either. After a long climb up the white spiral staircase, the guard knocked on a black door and then turned and left.

Confused, Julia turned to follow him, but he said something sharply in Sulallian and made a pushing gesture towards the door before continuing down the steps.

What does he mean? Julia wondered, studying the black wooden door in confusion as the guard disappeared down the steps. *Should I just open it?*

As she stood wondering, the door swung inwards, and Pallantu himself towered over her in his white mantle. His expression was grim.

"Sorry," was the first thing Julia managed to say. "I mean, I hope I'm not too late. I wanted to come right away, but Kasir said I was supposed to eat first, and I didn't want to embarrass him in front of everyone."

"No," Pallantu said darkly. "Instead, His Highness took the opportunity to embarrass me in front of everyone. But such is life. Come in, Julia. We have much to speak of, and little time."

He escorted her inside. Despite the size of the room, it felt closed in because of all the packed bookshelves and the tables and desks piled high with old tomes and various peculiar objects. But the regal man led her past all of these, to a pair of armchairs that stood turned towards one of the large, open windows.

"Do you call him His Highness?" Julia asked as they approached the chairs. "But he isn't really your prince, is he?"

Pallantu froze in mid-stride. His white-clad back stiffened, and Julia immediately regretted asking the question. She cleared her throat. "I mean, this is your world, right? And really, he's the prince of another world, Sulallia. But everyone here calls him Your Highness anyway."

Pallantu sighed and indicated one of the chairs. Julia seated herself.

"You are a very perceptive young woman," he said, sinking down into the chair across from her. "More perceptive than most. What you say is true."

Julia sunned herself in his compliment. It was such a welcome change to hear someone say that she was good at something – better than most, even – after all her failed tests.

Pallantu continued. "As you say, Paradisum is my domain. Even if it was Angelica who *created* it, it was I who perfected it after her tragic death – it is I who have led Paradisum's people, I who have gathered so many creators and artists here, I who have built this beautiful capital city. It is I who have given safety to all, and I who can win the war against the darkenwraiths. Here, I am the chief creator and the speaker of the Council. Here, my word is law. But not everyone respects the law." He met Julia's gaze, and she shifted uncomfortably in her chair.

"His Highness Kasir is not my prince," Pallantu continued. "But as the speaker of the Council, I am his guardian, until such time as he is ready to take his deceased father's crown. But that poor boy – it is hardly surprising he acts the way he does, considering the fact that his family once ruled a large, important domain. He is used to getting exactly what he wishes. Which makes his actions quite understandable, from a certain point of view."

"What actions?" Julia asked hesitantly.

"No, Julia," Pallantu said with a wave of his hand. "Do not think such things of your poor friend. His crimes are neither large nor particularly dangerous – not yet. But he defies me. He acts as if he were prince of Paradisum, and not merely of Sulallia. At present he is only a child, and not as perceptive a child as you. So he is fairly harmless. But he is popular. Popular as I have never been." He sighed. "Despite the fact that I have given the people safety and freedom and prosperity. Do you know how it feels, Julia, to do one's best, only to realise that one is thoroughly unappreciated anyway?"

Julia nodded. She wanted to lay a comforting hand on one of Pallantu's long, pale hands, but she refrained. A heavy silence followed. At last she said, "I failed all my tests yesterday. Everyone laughed at me, again and again – and then I was forced to have *Kasir* as some kind of tutor!"

Pallantu met her gaze. "My young friend," he said. "I am so sorry to hear of this indignity. It must have caused you great distress. But perhaps I can cheer you up with one piece of advice and two pieces of news. First, my advice." He cleared his throat. "Let Prince Kasir be your tutor. Be strong enough to bear this indignity and learn everything he has to teach you. For that is the path to victory."

"Victory?" said Julia.

"You will soon eclipse your friend," Pallantu said. "One day, people will speak of Julia Andersson and her great deeds, and they will forget all about Prince Kasir. Accepting his knowledge is one small step towards that goal. Tell me, my clever young friend, when Kasir gives you his knowledge, who becomes more powerful?"

Julia hesitated. "Me?"

"Precisely. For knowledge is power." Pallantu made a sweeping gesture towards the overfull bookshelves. "Here you see the secret to my power. Knowledge. Many creators believe that they are born with talent or that they receive it as some kind of gift – *inspiration*." He snorted. "But everything can be learned. Let Prince Kasir make you his equal in his narrow, limited field. Then you will become his superior all the faster."

Julia struggled to take in Pallantu's words. "You say that I'm going to be powerful," she said. "But I can't do anything at all! Everyone else is a magician with powers I can't even dream of, and I've failed every single test!"

"Not every test," Pallantu said, giving her a secretive smile. "And so we have arrived at my two pieces of news."

"Can you tell me when I can go home?" Julia asked eagerly.

A tiny grimace flashed across Pallantu's face, as if her question disappointed him deeply. But the expression vanished so quickly that Julia thought she might have imagined it. "Soon," he said. "Not today, but soon. Today's news is sufficient for today. However, my news has a price." He took a small box from the windowsill and passed it to Julia. "Open it, if you please."

Julia studied the little box. It was a beautiful piece of work, with sweeping curls of gold and silver over black wood with fine white inlays. Such a beautiful box must contain jewellery, she thought at first. But then she felt in some strange way that the box was not what it appeared to be. Something about it felt familiar, warm, like an old friend.

Pallantu cleared his throat, and Julia came back to reality and opened the box. The inside was lined with soft, black velvet. "It's empty," she said, confused.

Pallantu's eyes widened. "Empty," he repeated quietly. Golden rings gleamed in the sunlight as his right hand tightened its grip on the arm of his chair. Then he relaxed his grip and let out a little laugh. "I must congratulate you, my young friend. You have passed your second and greatest test. Which means that I can give you my two pieces of news."

"Test?" said Julia. "What do you mean? I just opened a little box."

"A box that only one other person has ever been able to open," said Pallantu. "I can assure you, Prince Kasir cannot open that box. He has tried."

"Can you?" Julia asked. "Or who's the other person?"

Pallantu cleared his throat. "I understand that this must be very confusing, and a lot to take in," he said. "We shall have to take things one step at a time. Today we start with the smallest step."

Julia was just about to shut the little box, but Pallantu hastily stuck a long, pale finger between the box and the lid, and then took it from her. He placed it on the windowsill with the lid open and then turned back to Julia. "You said that you had failed all of your tests," he said.

Julia avoided his gaze. "It was so humiliating. But they didn't have any test where you were just supposed to open little boxes."

"You only failed with regards to ordinary things," Pallantu said. "Sculpting, building, painting … Such arts can be learned by anyone who thinks they are worth the time. But you succeeded with something great, something that no one else at the Academy could have done – not even the instructors. I have been informed about what happened during the martial arts lesson."

Julia thought about how she had failed, how horrible she had been to her little brother and how she had almost got into a fight with the older girl. "Oh?" she said nervously. "What did you hear?"

"I heard that your brother failed."

Julia let out a small sigh of relief. "Is that all? Yes, well, he did well enough the time before that. Everyone thinks he's the greatest since he defeated Korak. Though it was really our dad's dagger that defeated him. And I think one of the girls in the class is actually better than Edvin."

"I am sure there are several students in the class who are better than Edvin at present," Pallantu said with a dismissive wave of his hand. "But he has great potential. I believe he can be a great help to you. But nevertheless, he failed. After succeeding so well the first time. Poor Harito was completely dumbfounded. In all his years of teaching, he has never seen someone fail that particular test after passing it once, and passing it so convincingly. He could not explain it."

"But everyone has off days, don't they?" Julia said.

Pallantu shook his head. "It was you," he said.

Julia's eyes widened. "Me?"

Pallantu nodded. "Most artists and creators have an innate knack for a certain art. Usually, it is something ordinary, such as singing or drawing or building or something like that. Each person has his or her own unique style of expression, but nevertheless, they tend to be variations of the same talents. Some have a particular affinity for two or more such arts. And sometimes, very rarely, an artist or a creator appears with an affinity for something out of the ordinary, something that is not taught at the Academy."

Julia gasped as comprehension dawned on her. Now she understood why she had felt as she had before Edvin had stuck the dagger into the dummy – and why she had felt so guilty afterward.

Pallantu nodded. "I see that you understand. You wanted your little brother to fail. You spoke, and you formed him with your power – you sculpted him like clay. And he failed. Despite his power, which is considerable, you were stronger."

"I can … make people fail?" said Julia. "Is it permanent?" The thought was terrifying, but also, in a horrible way, thrilling.

Pallantu shook his head slowly. "Your little brother should get back his powers soon if it has not already happened. And if he has not, you should be able to give them back to him."

"So I can make people strong, too?" said Julia.

"Probably," said Pallantu. "But you must be careful with that aspect of your gift." He raised a warning finger, and the ruby on one of his rings caught the sunlight. "It can be dangerous to make others strong," he continued. "Sometimes more dangerous than making them weak."

Julia considered his words. Actually, she wasn't really sure what he meant at all, but he had called her clever, so she didn't want to embarrass herself by asking. Instead she changed the subject. "You said that you had two things to tell me."

"Quite right," said Pallantu. "Your talent is, as I said, very rare. But it is most likely related to wordcraft. So you are to have a tutor – one who is much more powerful and experienced than your friend Prince Kasir. You are to study under the city's greatest wordcrafter."

Julia felt a thrill pass through her entire body. She could hardly contain herself. "You don't mean …?"

Pallantu nodded. "As often as I can spare the time, I will instruct you. But speaking of time …" He rose to his feet and strode towards the door, and Julia hurried after him. "Unfortunately, that is all the time we have today."

"But I have so many questions!" Julia protested. "When can I go home? Or when can you tell me? And do you know what's happened to Lars-Petter? I haven't seen him! And …"

"Another time," Pallantu said, herding her out through the door. "I will tell you more next time."

The door closed, and Julia stood there, locked outside of Pallantu's study, alone with her questions.

21

Julia was not looking forward to the humiliation of her drawing lesson. But with everything Pallantu had told her, she felt she could steel herself against it. Because really, she was stronger than the others, even if they didn't know it. She had a talent that none of them had. And if they weren't kind to her – then perhaps she could use her talent to get back at them.

Pallantu's guard left her by the main entrance to the Academy, where she was left to her own devices to guess where she was supposed to go. Since it did not yet feel like lunch time, she made her way to the same classroom where she had done her drawing test the day before. Sure enough, she found the teacher and the class, including Kasir.

The teacher said something to her in Sulallian when she came in through the door, but it was Kasir who answered. A short conversation between Kasir and the teacher ensued. Julia stood in the doorway the whole time, shifting uncomfortably, unsure if she should take a seat or leave the room, or what she was supposed to do. The entire situation aggravated her.

At last Kasir rose and escorted her out of the room. "We go," he said. "Drawing, you and me."

Julia nodded silently and followed him. As they walked along the white marble corridor, she thought about Pallantu's advice. *Let him teach you what he can. Let him make you stronger.*

When they had turned a corner, Kasir suddenly confronted her with eager intensity. "Pallantu say with you. What?"

Julia was completely taken aback. "I … he's going to be my tutor," she stammered.

Kasir stared. "Pallantu?" he said. "You?"

Julia glared at him. "What, you don't think that I'm good enough to be taught by the city's greatest creator? You aren't the only one who has talents, Kasir!"

The boy's eyes widened. He shook his head. "No, you not understand. Pallantu … Not listen. Bad. Pallantu … Pallantu say you. What?"

Julia stared at Kasir, trying to decide if his words contained some insult. She suddenly thought of everything Pallantu had said about the boy. That he didn't respect the law, that he was used to being in control and getting what he wanted. Could he be dangerous? "Pallantu didn't say all that much," she lied. "He had so little time … because I came *late*. But he said that he would give me private lessons."

Kasir shook his head and led her onward.

At last they arrived at the cavernous wooden room full of desks. Thankfully, Doneus wasn't there, but a number of students sat working on various projects. As the private lesson began, Julia became painfully aware of the fact that their voices were the only ones to be heard in the otherwise silent room. She felt embarrassed by Kasir's accent and his atrocious Swedish. Then she realised how absurd this was. No one else could understand a word of what they were saying anyway.

Kasir tried to get her to draw a series of intricate curlicues, which he drew quickly and effortlessly before telling her to copy them. Copying his patterns was not all that difficult; the only problem was that his began to move on the paper as soon as he had drawn them. Hers remained completely still. Now and then, Kasir said something about how she was supposed to feel or think while she drew. But with his Swedish, she could hardly understand what he meant, and most of it seemed to be nonsense anyway.

It wasn't long before Julia got frustrated. She was sorely tempted to use her power to make Kasir fail with a few curlicues. But just as she thought this, she noticed the Troubadour's lute lying in the waste basket. The sight of it made her so sad that her desire to get back at Kasir vanished. But not quite sad enough to pick the instrument up and place it back on his desk.

After a while, Kasir also began to lose his patience. It was hard to say if he was more frustrated with her or with his own inability to explain what he meant in

Swedish. But regardless, it just made her angrier until they were so cross with each other that it became unbearable.

Kasir sighed, pushed his chair back and stood. "Break," he said. "Come."

"You can't just say 'come' to me, like a dog!" Julia said, offended. "Just because you're supposed to give me lessons doesn't mean that you're my teacher. And you're not my prince either. If you want to push people around and tell them what to do, you can go do it in your own world!"

Kasir's eyes widened, and he gaped. Then he spun on his heel and left the room without a word.

Horrified, Julia realised what she had said. Kasir couldn't go home. His world had been destroyed by the darkenwraiths. She hurried after him.

"Kasir!" she cried, ignoring the looks that the other students gave her. "Kasir! I'm sorry! I didn't mean it!"

The boy's narrow shoulders rose and fell, and he stopped in the middle of the corridor ahead of her with his head bowed.

"Kasir?" She approached him hesitantly.

He didn't look up to meet her gaze.

"It was a stupid thing to say," she said. "Really stupid. I wasn't thinking! I'm so sorry, Kasir! I'm sorry!"

He stared determinedly down at the marble floor.

"I know that you can't go home," Julia continued. "I can't go home either. I know that it's hard. And I know that you're a prince from a great world. I'm sorry if I haven't shown you the proper respect. If you want me to call you Your Highness …"

Kasir shook his head. "Not your highest. Not world. Not Sulallia. Not home! Not! No! Gone!"

He looked up, his eyes brimming with tears. Not knowing what else to do, Julia laid an arm around his shoulders. Kasir let the arm remain for a moment. Then he dried his eyes and met her gaze.

"Break," he said. "Break. Take Edvin. Go out."

Julia followed him to the martial arts classroom. There they found a very despondent Edvin sitting on a bench and watching the other students throw knives.

"What's wrong, Edvin?" Julia asked, sitting down beside him.

He sighed deeply. "I can't do it," he said, waving his hand in the general direction of his classmates.

"What do you mean?" said Julia.

"I can't do anything," said Edvin. "Somehow I managed to impress everyone the first time, but now I'm just bad at everything. I'm still in the class, but I can't do anything."

A pang of guilt gripped Julia's heart. "I'm sure you're just having a bad day," she said. "Everyone has bad days. But you're really good at this – everyone knows it. You have a gift. Let's go out and take a break, and when we come back, everyone's going to be amazed at how good you are." As she spoke, she felt a peculiar warmth spread from her heart down to her stomach and then out to her whole body. In some strange way, it felt as if the warmth washed over Edvin, and when he looked up, his gaze was suddenly full of hope.

"Do you really think so?" he asked.

"Absolutely," Julia said, smiling. "You're the best." Pallantu's warning about making others stronger flashed through her mind, but she pushed it away. The smile on her little brother's face was worth whatever dangers Pallantu might have been referring to. "I can't think of anyone better to use Dad's dagger," she said. In a way, it was hard for her to say the words, but in another way it felt wonderful, and she saw the effect they had on Edvin. He sat straighter, and the glumness left his face.

Then he suddenly hung his head. "Lalora's better than me," he said. "She took Dad's dagger. And the teacher hasn't done anything about it."

Julia's gaze followed his pointing finger and saw the tall, bronze-skinned girl who she had almost got into a fight with the day before. Now Lalora stood in the center of a ring of students, kicking at leather cushions that they held in their hands. Her kicks were swift and powerful, and she moved so quickly that it was hard to follow her movements. But then she suddenly stopped in front of two students who held a wooden board between them, and Julia saw a silver handle stuck in her black cloth belt. The dagger! She rose to go and confront the girl. At that moment, Lalora performed a final kick, and the wooden board broke in half with a loud crack. The other students cheered.

Julia froze, staring. It was no thin, flimsy board the girl had broken. Then she reminded herself of her great power and strode forward.

"You have something that belongs to my brother!" she said, stepping into the ring.

Lalora stared at her, and Julia suddenly remembered that the girl couldn't understand a word she said. But she thought about her power and continued. "How dare you take my dad's dagger? My brother defeated Korak with it. But you? Well, you do all right against dummies and wooden boards, but soon you're not even going to manage that. You weak, pathetic little …"

The girl approached with long, confident strides, stopping uncomfortably close and towering over her. Julia stood her ground and stretched out her hand. "My brother's dagger," she said.

Lalora threw her head back and laughed.

Then Kasir stepped into the ring, speaking sternly in Sulallian. Lalora stared at him and hesitated for a tense moment. Then she bowed slightly, drew the dagger and held it out toward Julia.

Just as she was about to take it, the older girl dropped the weapon so it landed, point downward, and buried itself in the wooden floor about a millimetre from Julia's foot. She jumped. Then she bent down with burning cheeks and picked up the dagger. When she straightened up again, the look Lalora gave her was deadlier than any dagger – but not as deadly as the look that Kasir gave Lalora.

Without paying the older girl any mind, Julia turned on her heel and handed the dagger back to Edvin.

"Thanks," Edvin mumbled, accepting the weapon. Then he lifted his gaze. "Julia, you're shaking."

"That girl just makes me so angry," Julia said, trying to convince herself that that was all it was. "Come on," she said. "Let's go take a break." She led the boys toward the exit.

Kasir said something in Sulallian to one of the teachers on the way out, and the woman didn't seem to have any objections. Or if she had any, Julia didn't understand them.

The other teacher, the short, bronze-skinned man who had tested Julia the day before, did not look happy at all. He stopped instructing his group and glared at them as they crossed the floor toward the door. Julia tried to ignore him, but it was almost as if his gaze burned its way into her back. She shivered. It was only when they had emerged into the corridor that she was struck by how much he resembled Lalora. The same eyes, the same nose … Could they be related?

"Where are we going?" Edvin asked, as Kasir led the way through the corridors.

"Out," said Kasir. "See Pallantor. See … Out."

22

They took quite a long break. Pallantor was a large city, and Kasir seemed to want to show them all of it. They visited a neighborhood of wooden houses painted in vivid colours. This part of the city was a considerable contrast to what Julia had seen of Pallantor so far, with all its stately, sombre pillars of white marble.

When they had left the colourful houses behind, they passed through something like a combination of a carnival and a zoo. Small black tents housed games consisting of spinning wheels, thrown balls and peculiar brass contraptions. Exotic creatures like something out of a dream lounged in beautifully crafted cages under white tents. After the tents, they arrived at a cobblestone square surrounded by enormous, temple-like buildings with prominent pillars. The square was packed with people and yet eerily quiet as the solemn crowd drifted silently among its bronze sculptures – the only sound Julia heard was Edvin asking questions about everything.

At last they arrived at a lively marketplace that seemed to be their destination. Food, drink, toys, tools and objects whose use Julia could not imagine were being sold among street performers and colourful crowds.

In the midst of the market's chaos, a network of small parks connected by raised wooden bridges served as green oases of calm. They stopped in one of these parks and sat in the grass by a cheerfully bubbling artificial stream. To Julia's surprise, Kasir took off his shoes and dipped his feet in the water with a sigh. Edvin followed his example, and at last Julia also followed suit. The cool water on her toes was extremely refreshing after the long walk. It was also nice to get away from all of Kasir's fans. Even in the silent square, a steady stream of admirers had bowed quietly as he walked past.

Julia lay back on the grass and closed her eyes, letting the din of the marketplace wash over her. A sorrowful melody played on a lone flute rose above the lively sounds of the crowd. *A street performer*, she thought.

A wonderful combination of scents wafted over from the marketplace: sweet, spicy, and the smell of something fried. Julia found herself daydreaming about food and wondered lazily if it might be time to eat lunch at the Academy.

Apparently, Edvin was thinking the same thing. "I'm starving," he said. "Can't we buy one of those fried things on a stick, or some of those green noodles or something?"

"Buy with what?" Julia said. At once she felt exactly like her own mother. That was the way Mum often answered her when the Fall Market came to town and she wanted to buy some unique cap or an absurdly large apple-flavoured candy cane.

"Oh, right," said Edvin. "We don't have any money. Though I guess you could sell that mirror if we need some."

"Sell Dad's mirror?" Julia sat bolt upright and thrust her hand into the pocket of her white tunic, feeling the silver mirror's handle as if to reassure herself that it was still there. Since her experience the night before, she was reluctant to leave it in her room. "Never!" she said. "How could you even think something like that? Next you'll want to sell the dagger too, I suppose?"

"No, you're right, it was a silly thing to say," said Edvin. "But if we need money to survive, we should probably sell the mirror first. The dagger is at least useful if we have to fight."

"There are more important things in life than fighting," said Julia. "And we don't need any money to survive. Our food is waiting for us at school."

"But what if we miss lunch?" Edvin complained. He turned to Kasir. "You're a prince, right? I mean, you're a prince, aren't you, Your Highness?"

"Not highest," Kasir said, shaking his head. "They" – he waved his hand in a gesture encompassing the entire city – "you highest, you highest, you highest. Not friend. Zero friend." He formed a zero with his fingers. "Only you highest. Edvin and Julia friend. Not you highest. Friend say Kasir."

"Fine," said Edvin. "Kasir. You're a prince. Don't you have any money? You know, money we can buy food with?"

Kasir shook his head slowly. Then his face suddenly lit up. "I get," he said. "I get! Wait." He rose and wiped his feet on the grass before thrusting them, still wet, into his shoes.

"Wait for me!" said Edvin. "I want to come along!" He stood up.

"Don't forget your shoes!" Julia said before he could disappear with Kasir. "You don't want someone to steal them." That was also the sort of thing Mum would say if they left any toys or anything out in the garden. Which was actually completely absurd. As if anyone would want to steal their broken old things.

"But can't you keep an eye on them?" Edvin asked.

"I'm resting," said Julia. "I didn't come here to watch shoes."

With a sigh, Edvin picked up his shoes and hurried after Kasir without bothering to put them on.

Julia settled down on the grass again, enjoying the water, the music and the smells. The delicious aromas were a hundred times more heavenly now that she knew she would be eating soon. Kasir would take care of it. Although … What was he actually going to get? Food, or money? One couldn't really just "get" money. With rising anxiety, Julia once again thought about what Pallantu had said about Kasir not respecting the law.

To distract herself, she sat up and pulled out the little hand mirror. *What kind of magical powers do you have?* she wondered, studying its silvery surface. But of course she only saw her own reflection. The wind had not been kind to her hair today. The park behind her looked nice, at least, she thought as she tried in vain to comb her hair with her fingers. In the mirror she saw the light green grass, the dark green bushes, the trees with their waxy leaves and purple flowers. She saw all the way to the little stone wall surrounding the park, and beyond it, to the teeming crowds of the market.

The flute player sat on the stone wall, a large man wrapped in a purple cloak, with a black, wide-brimmed hat. He rocked from side to side as he played. Something in his reflection looked familiar.

Julia almost dropped the mirror when she suddenly realised who he was. She hurried barefoot over the grass towards him. "Lars-Petter!" she said as she reached the stone wall.

The flute player stiffened but quickly resumed rocking in time with his own music as if he hadn't heard. Julia stepped over the little stone wall to look him in the face. He was wearing a black mask of polished wood. The mask looked like an exaggerated laugh, with squinting eye holes and a broad, smiling mouth. Could this really be Lars-Petter? Her doubts grew as he continued to play.

"Lars-Petter?" she said hesitantly, leaning closer. The man gave off a pungent odour that might be some kind of alcohol.

He stopped playing abruptly. "Don't say that name!" he hissed.

The small crowd that had gathered to listen began muttering. The flute player rose to his feet, bowed deeply and said something in Sulallian. Then he took up his wooden begging bowl, jumped over the stone wall and loped unsteadily across the park.

"Wait!" Julia cried, running after him. "I need to talk with you!"

The man staggered to a halt and turned to face her. "Why?" he said. "Why does Henrik Andersson's daughter need to talk to me? Don't you know who I am? How did you recognise me, anyway? I was playing unrecognisability over myself. I must be both drunk and worthless if you could see through me."

"You're … drunk?" said Julia.

The Troubadour bowed with an exaggerated flourish. "Yes, that I am, little girl. And soon I'm going to the tavern to get even drunker. And tomorrow I'm going to beg for more money and get drunk again, and the next day I'll do the same thing, and then the day after that and the day after that. I'm the Troubadour, the crazy, dangerous drunk. I'm everything your mother ever warned you about and worse. It's all my fault. Everything. All the–" His voice broke, and he didn't finish his thought.

"It can't be as bad as all that," Julia said hesitantly.

"If you only knew, girl. It's my fault that you're here … Where are you, anyway?"

"Here." Julia waved.

"No, I'm not that drunk. I mean, where are you staying now? Are you and Edvin still at the Academy, or … No, you know what, you should never answer that kind of question when a stranger or a dangerous drunk asks it. Forget it. Pallantu will take care of you now. Just like he plans to take care of everything." He laughed bitterly.

"Lars-Petter," Julia said, fixing her gaze on the mask's eye holes. "I don't know what's happened to you, but you're not a stranger, and you're not a dangerous drunk either. You're my dad's friend. You're a great creator and a hero! You've saved me and Edvin and Kasir. Where would we be without you?"

"Not in this awful place," Lars-Petter muttered. He reeled to one side and then righted himself. "Just promise me one thing," he said.

"What?"

"Don't trust Pallantu. He can help you. He's powerful. But don't let him get you entangled in anything, don't let him use you. Make sure that he solves your problems and sends you home at once. And then forget him. And me. And all of this."

Julia didn't know how she was supposed to respond. She changed the subject. "How have things gone for Dawn?" she asked.

"Dawn?" Lars-Petter laughed bitterly. "Things have gone just as well for her as for everyone I'm supposed to take care of. It's all the same – all of it. Every time. Good-bye, Julia. And sorry." He staggered off, jumped over the artificial stream, and then plunged into the crowd on the other side. He raised the flute to his lips and played a few notes, and suddenly Julia couldn't see him anymore. She stopped at the edge of the marketplace.

"It's not true!" she shouted after him. "It's not your fault! You saved us! You can save Dawn!"

A few people in the crowd turned and stared at her, and she fell silent. She didn't even know whether Lars-Petter was still within earshot. With a sigh, she turned back to the artificial stream. Then she searched for the place where she had rested before, where she had left her shoes. But they were nowhere to be found.

Julia didn't tell the others about her encounter with Lars-Petter when they returned. Partially because she didn't know how to tell them that he had started drinking again. But perhaps a larger part was that she suddenly felt entangled in the thorny question of whom she was supposed to trust. Lars-Petter said that she shouldn't trust Pallantu. But he was drunk and bore a grudge against the man. Pallantu said that Kasir didn't respect the law, and he hinted that he might be dangerous.

"How did you get these, anyway?" Julia asked as they sat eating fried bits of meat on sticks and drinking sweet juice out of blue coconut shells.

"We sort of went to the bank," said Edvin. "We went into this really big building, and Kasir got some money."

Julia gave the boys a probing look. "Got money?" she said. "You didn't rob the bank, did you?"

"No," said Edvin. He sounded disappointed. "We got to cut to the front of the queue when they saw it was Kasir, but then he just said something – I heard the word 'three', and then they gave him three little coins. We used them to pay for the food. It was pretty boring, actually. I should have stayed here with you. But at least I learned what these things are called." He pointed to the last piece of meat on his stick and babbled something.

Kasir corrected his pronunciation. On the third try, the young prince seemed satisfied. Julia didn't bother trying to imitate them.

Once they had eaten, Kasir said it was time to go back to the Academy. They rose to their feet, and the boys put on their shoes.

"Are you really going to walk barefoot like that?" Edvin asked as they set off. "Where are your shoes, anyway?"

"Forget it," Julia said. "Please, just forget it."

23

Thankfully, Maja had packed several pairs of shoes for Julia. Unfortunately, they were in a chest up in her room, and she had to traverse a rather large amount of public corridor to get there. A number of students pointed at her bare feet, whispering to each other and giggling as she and the boys passed. And then, after they had turned a corner, she saw Doneus' stately figure headed towards them.

"Walk in front of me," she urged, placing herself so that Edvin and Kasir stood between her and the older student.

"Why?" Edvin asked, confused.

Don't see me, don't see me, Julia thought desperately.

Doneus saw them and brightened. He bowed to Kasir and said something in Sulallian, and Kasir nodded in reply and returned his greeting. Then the older student exchanged greetings with Edvin. At last his steady, green-eyed gaze landed on Julia.

Julia's heart stopped, and she shifted slightly to try to hide her bare feet behind Edvin, who gave her a confused look. Doneus smiled and bowed. "Mynamus Jolia," he said.

"Just Julia," she answered clumsily. "I mean, hi, Doneus." She felt her cheeks getting hot and remembered that he didn't understand a word she was saying. But Kasir said a few words that might have been an explanation – she heard the word "Julia", at least – and Doneus smiled at her again and said something in Sulallian before continuing on his way.

When he had gone, Edvin burst out laughing. "You like him!" he said. "Don't you, Julia! You like Doneus!"

Julia snorted. "Don't be absurd." But when they had reached the stairs, she couldn't contain herself any longer. "What did he say, Kasir?" she asked. "Before he left? He said something to me, didn't he?"

Kasir furrowed his brow. "Hard," he said. "Maybe … boot? Bootful … flower?"

Julia felt as if she might faint. "Did he really say that? That I'm as beautiful as a flower?"

Kasir screwed up his face as if thinking intensely. "Like … bootful foot flower?" He pointed at her right foot.

Julia looked down and saw that a purple flower petal from the park had stuck to the side of her foot. Her heart sank.

Edvin laughed.

Luckily, Doneus was nowhere to be seen when Julia and Kasir arrived at the room with all the desks. And the break seemed to have done them good, for now they resumed the interrupted lesson without argument or frustration. Maybe the fresh air and freedom

213

had helped Julia get rid of some stress. Or maybe she was too worried about the Troubadour to feel frustrated with Kasir or with herself.

As she copied Kasir's swirling figures, her thoughts strayed to Lars-Petter. Where was he now? She hoped he hadn't gone and got even drunker as he had said. It was such a shame things had turned out this way, after the change she had seen in him in Maja's world. She thought about what Maja had said about the Troubadour, that he was a powerful creator, that he could probably make a whole world of his own if he wanted to.

She also said that I could become a creator. Or that I was a creator or at least a reflection of the Great Creator or something … She thought about the raspberry she had painted with Maja's help.

"Good! Good! Good, Julia!"

Julia awoke from her reverie and discovered that one of the curls she had drawn was shivering on the page, like a vibrating string. As she watched, it slowly stopped trembling.

"It worked," she said, staring at the drawing. "It worked!" She turned to Kasir and threw her arms around him. "I did it! You did it! You taught me! You're the best!" As the words left her lips, a peculiar warmth grew in her heart – the same warmth as when she had tried to restore Edvin's talent. Her gaze gravitated to the waste basket.

She released Kasir and dug the broken lute out of the rubbish. "Kasir," she said, laying the instrument on his desk. "Maja was right about you. You're a fantastic creator. You can draw things that come to life, and now you've taught me to do it too. I think you can fix this."

Kasir stared at the instrument. He shook his head slowly.

"Come on, you can do this! I know you can!" As Julia spoke, she felt how the warmth spread to Kasir. Then, slowly, he nodded.

"Why don't we do it like this?" Julia said excitedly. "We'll make it a race and see if you can fix the lute before I can make ten drawings move."

Kasir considered. "Maybe …" he said.

"Great!" said Julia. "Ready, set, go!" She put her pen to the paper and began working furiously on a new curlicue.

Kasir stiffened. "Wait! Wait!" he said. "Cheat!" He began rummaging in the drawers of his desk, perhaps looking for the right paints or brushes.

Julia laughed.

It wasn't easy to get the pictures to move. She had to fill two sheets of paper with curls before the next one came to life, but once it started moving, it coiled and uncoiled itself like a snake, with larger, more violent movements than the first. Kasir smiled at Julia's ecstatic pride, but then he immediately became engrossed in his own work again.

After five sheets of paper, Julia had managed to get four drawings to move. The fourth slithered all the way to the edge of the paper and vanished. Julia stared.

"Kasir?" she said.

He grunted without looking up.

"I got a fourth one," she said. "But it sort of … disappeared."

"Good," said Kasir. "Draw, draw. Draw good."

Julia shrugged and continued. Now it was getting easier. The next sheet of paper gave her a fifth living drawing, even if it was a bit more subdued than the others, and on the next sheet, she managed to achieve two quite energetic curls. Only three left to win.

She glanced at Kasir, who sat studying the lute with his brow furrowed. Now it was whole, but he didn't seem to be satisfied. As she watched, he wiped away a bit of it with his finger, and a section of the hole reappeared. She turned back to her drawing. The next curlicue danced cheerfully on the paper as soon as she had finished drawing it. But it took a while before she could get a ninth drawing to move. Perhaps the stress and excitement of being so close to victory made it harder. After what felt like far too many tries, she finally managed to get a ninth curl to vibrate a little.

"Nine!" she said proudly.

Kasir answered by strumming a finished, fully repaired lute.

Julia laughed. A part of her thought that she should be cross because Kasir had won. But another part of her, a larger part, felt the same warmth as when she had spoken the encouraging words that had given him power. His victory was her victory.

For the rest of the day, Julia was in a good mood – until something suddenly landed on her tunic as she sat eating dinner. She looked down and saw a dark red mass of something like red beet salad rolling down the white cloth. It left a long, pink stain.

She looked up and was met by a contemptuous smile on a bronze-skinned face at the next table over. Lalora.

"Don't look at her," Edvin whispered. "She's not in a good mood today." He passed her a cloth serviette.

Julia's anger flashed to life as she tried to wipe the pink stain away. She only managed to spread it around. Hullevin passed her his water glass, whistling something in Sulallian.

"I think he wants you to dip your serviette in his water," said Edvin.

"Could you thank him for me?" said Julia.

Edvin whistled something while Julia poured a few drops of water on the serviette to get it damp. The water helped a little, but regardless of how much she rubbed the cloth, she couldn't achieve more than a wet, very watered-down pink stain. Lalora was laughing at something along with the girls at her table. Julia was glad she couldn't understand them. She thought about the horse girls back home in Klippsby, and she clenched her teeth.

"Did you say she was in a bad mood today?" she asked when she had regained her composure enough to speak again. "Did class go badly for her, or what?" She remembered the words she had used on the girl while reclaiming the dagger.

Edvin shook his head. "No, today she was the best, as always. It's just that she didn't like it when you took the dagger back. I …" He hesitated. "I left it in my room afterwards, and just used the knives they have there. Not that I'm afraid of her or anything, but …"

"I understand." Julia patted his shoulder. His news about the girl's success was disappointing. Hadn't Julia's power worked? "But how did things go for you today, without the dagger?" she asked.

Edvin brightened. "Really great, actually," he said. "Better than ever, I think. Hullevin and I—" He suddenly fell silent.

The rest of the cafeteria had also gone silent. Julia turned and saw a towering figure standing in the doorway, holding a poleaxe.

24

During the brisk walk to Pallantu's tower, Julia tried every trick she could to hide the pink stain. *Typical that it would happen just as I'm about to meet the most powerful man in the city*, she thought. A sudden mental image of Lalora's contemptuous smile made her blood boil.

At last, she arrived at a solution, folding the cloth inward and holding it in place by walking with her hands in her pockets. That would have to do. It might look a bit strange, but hopefully not quite as embarrassing as the pink stain.

Unfortunately, Pallantu was not deceived. "Have you spilled on yourself?" he asked once she had reached his tower and they had seated themselves in the chairs by the window.

Julia looked away from his raised eyebrow. "I, ummm …"

Pallantu caught her eye with a grave look. "Come now, Julia. You have no need to hide anything from me. I am not the kind of man one should try to hide things from; I tend to see them anyway. But you have nothing to be ashamed of. In this tower, you can be yourself."

Julia sighed and took her hands out of her pockets. The white cloth unfolded, revealing the pink stain. "It was a girl at the Academy," she said.

Pallantu nodded sadly. "Some people have a way of being terribly unpleasant, especially towards those who are different. And those who have great potential. But here, I believe I can help you."

He waved his hand, and a blue gem on one of his rings flashed. The stain vanished.

Julia gaped at the front of her tunic. "It's clean!" she said.

Pallantu gave her a faint smile. "Actually, that is not entirely true," he said. "But it *looks* clean, and that is what really matters, is it not?"

Julia hesitated. "Well, I guess," she said, laughing a little.

"And the girl who did this to you," Pallantu continued. "What did you do to her?"

"Nothing! She just took Edvin's dagger, and I tried to get it back, and Kasir told her off, and …"

Pallantu sighed. "Envy," he said. "She knows whose children you are. Let me guess. We are talking about the kind of person who is overly proud of her own skills? Yes, I see that I have guessed correctly. I think that I could even tell you who she is and whose daughter she is. But do not let yourself be bothered by such people, Julia. What did you do to her afterward?"

"Nothing!" said Julia. Then she felt the weight of Pallantu's gaze and remembered what he had said about hiding things. "Oh, all right. I told her that she was weak, and that she couldn't do anything. I tried to make her fail … But it didn't seem to work."

"Interesting," said Pallantu. "Very interesting. Did you use an interpreter?"

"No, but … Do you think someone has to understand what I say for my power to work on them?"

"It would not surprise me."

"Hmmm … It worked with Edvin and Kasir, but of course they …"

Pallantu fixed her with a look that made her fall silent. "Did you make them stronger?" he demanded.

"Well, I know you said I should be careful about that," Julia pleaded. "But Edvin's my brother, and Kasir's my friend."

"Sometimes it is our friends who we have to be most careful with," said Pallantu. "It is they who can hurt us the most. Oh well, it is probably just as well that you made your brother stronger. We are likely to have use of his power. But speaking of power, I have called you here to give you knowledge. Unfortunately, we shall have to act faster than I had hoped."

"Does this mean I can go home soon?"

"Yes," said Pallantu. "If you desire it. And if we succeed. Which, of course, we will."

"Succeed at what?"

Pallantu rose from his chair and fetched something from a nearby desk. It was the same small, empty box that she had opened before – still open.

"Now I shall tell you about this baffling little creation and why I asked you to open it," said Pallantu. "It was a gift from your father."

Julia studied the box with a new appreciation. She brushed its polished surface with her fingertips. Pallantu stiffened. "I'm not going to close it," Julia said hurriedly.

Pallantu let out a little laugh. "Of course not. Anyway, when your father gave me this little puzzle, he said that no one could open it except for him."

"Why would he give you a box that you couldn't open?"

"A box that he *said* I could not open," Pallantu corrected. "Perhaps it was one of his many jokes, perhaps a challenge. Perhaps he simply wanted to test me and see if I could work out some solution."

"Why not just ask him to open it?" Julia asked. "If you were friends, why not let him open it for you? Then his hand would be like your hand, if you see what I mean?" She thought of the joy she had felt when Kasir had won their competition.

Pallantu opened his mouth, then closed it again. He shook his head and sighed. "Life is complicated, Julia. Very, very complicated. But now I have done something similar. I have opened it with the hand of his daughter. Which shows that one of my theories was correct: he tied the box to his blood in some way. So I have solved his puzzle, even if it took me sixteen years. I have not called you here to talk about this box, however. The matter at hand is something much greater: a chest that must be opened at all costs, but which no one has the power to open. Except for you, and possibly your brother."

"Did my dad make that chest, too?"

Pallantu nodded.

"What's in it?"

"I call it the Darkenstar," said Pallantu. "Whether the darkenwraiths have their own name for it, I do not know. But it is a terrible weapon, one which your father, Angelica and Lars-Petter managed to take from the darkenwraiths a long time ago, before it was ever used. Unfortunately, Angelica lost her life in the attempt, but her sacrifice was necessary. If the darkenwraiths were to get ahold of the Darkenstar, I believe they would be able to steal the powers of any creator they wished. They would even gain the power to leave Thousandworld – to escape into worlds such as your own and desolate them as well."

Julia stiffened. "But they've already managed to get into my world," she gasped.

"Precisely," said Pallantu. "And that is why we must act quickly. Korak has managed to send a part of himself out into your world, but not his full power. Which suggests he has found some way of making contact with the Darkenstar, but he has not yet managed to open the chest fully."

Julia's thoughts spun. "But that means he has the chest!"

Pallantu nodded. "When your father had taken the Darkenstar, he hid it in the safest place we could think of. The chest is built into the throne room in Sulallia."

"But the darkenwraiths have taken Sulallia!"

"Correct. We underestimated their strength. And so we must recover the Darkenstar from its current location and hide it in the only place where it can be truly safe – the city that is mightier than Sulallia ever was, where the best creators in Thousandworld's thousand domains have gathered for common defence. We must bring it here, to Pallantor."

"But how?" said Julia. "I heard that no one's ever defeated Korak. Or, well, Edvin, but that was just a part of Korak or something. It must be really dangerous to go to Sulallia and try to … Wait a minute, you don't mean that *I'm* supposed to go there and face him?"

Pallantu met her gaze, and a long silence followed. Julia's cheeks burned, but her stomach felt cold. Then Pallantu stood, went to the window and looked out over the sunset beyond the city's white spires. "Your father was a very brave man," he said at last. "A true hero, willing to face any danger and endure any hardship to save those in need of saving. A bit like your little brother, Edvin, who dared to fight Korak to save his sister's life."

Julia didn't answer. Her hand stroked the smooth surface of the box nervously.

"He was willing to sacrifice everything, your father, to make sure that the darkenwraiths never gained the power to enter your world, the power to harm the ones he loved there. Your mother, for example."

Julia leaped up out of her seat. "They don't want to hurt Mum, do they? But they've already been to our house! I have to get home and—"

Pallantu raised a hand, and she fell silent. "Korak cannot harm her yet," he assured her. "He used too much of his power in the hunt for you and your brother. He cannot escape Thousandworld again. Not yet. But if he is allowed too much time to work on the chest, if he manages to improve his contact with the Darkenstar … Julia, stopping him and saving your world requires great courage. It requires people with the same heroic heart as your father. People like your little brother, for example."

Julia felt something burning within her, something like rage, but different. A growing determination.

"But how?" she said at last. "If no one has ever been able to defeat Korak …"

"Korak has never faced me," Pallantu said. He met her gaze, and his eyes flashed with cold power, like the sapphire in his ring. "I have trained and studied for this moment for many years. I have gathered power from the mightiest creators in Thousandworld, and now I am the mightiest. Who do you think has seen to it that the darkenwraiths can never set foot in this city? Here everyone is safe, for I am here. And if someone were brave enough to accompany me on a brief visit to Sulallia, she would be perfectly safe, because I would be there. Do you trust me?"

Julia hesitated. But what he said about Pallantor was true. She had been completely safe during her stay in the city, despite the fact that Korak was after her. Besides, Pallantu had been a friend of her dad's.

"When do you want to go?" she said at last.

Pallantu closed his eyes. "Thank you." He fell to his knees. "Thank you, you courageous daughter of my precious friend! Now I see his heroism in you." When he opened his eyes again, they gleamed with tears. "You are marvellous," he went on. "Everything I thought about you has been proven true, and more – a true hero, a true creator!" He wiped his eyes and rose to his feet.

"You asked when I intend to depart," he continued. All his sentimentality had vanished as quickly as it had come, but Julia still felt as if she were floating. "Actually, I wanted to wait. I wanted to give you more time, to wait until you were ready. But it is not only Korak's actions that have made the matter more urgent. The Council has forced my hand. They want to compel me to close the portal to Sulallia."

Julia gaped. "But why? If Korak's getting more and more of the Darkenstar's power … And how can they force you to do anything? Aren't you in charge?"

"First among equals," Pallantu said, shaking his head. "I have always believed in the Council, never taken power into my own hands as I could. But their cowardice, their treachery – this has come as a total surprise. I could never have imagined that they would throw away our only possibility of salvation. But then, I am not the one who chose them. Not Angelica or your father, either, and neither of them ever trusted all the councilmembers completely. Anyway, they seemed to be in full agreement with my plan to recover the Darkenstar, until our meeting two hours ago. Now everything has changed. Now they are suddenly too frightened. They fear that the darkenwraiths could use the portal to attack us here in Paradisum. Safety at any price, they think – even if it means the destruction of all other worlds."

"But they can't do that!" Julia protested. "They can't force you to close the portal against your will!"

"I am afraid they can," Pallantu said with a sigh. "Such is the nature of democracy." He raised his hands and let them fall. "Not all of us are princes with the freedom to do exactly as they please. However …" He smiled at Julia. "The Council has accepted my petition for time; I have three days to close the portal. Which means that …"

"We have to leave soon!" Julia said eagerly.

"Tomorrow," said Pallantu. "We shall have to leave tomorrow. But first, I intend to train you – to train you properly."

25

It was a long, intense lesson, and it lasted until late at night. Pallantu sent for several people for Julia to practise on. She made his bodyguard weak and then strong again – but not too strong, for Pallantu interrupted her. She weakened a young woman's ability to sing and a poet's ability to recite living poems. Everything worked in Pallantu's presence, because everyone could understand what she said. Personally, Julia wanted to experiment with saying some encouraging or weakening words that Pallantu would write down in Sulallian. Maybe it would be enough if she just showed someone the paper. But Pallantu said they were in a hurry and had no time for such experiments.

"But what do I do if I get separated from you?" asked Julia.

Pallantu gave her an inscrutable look. "Do not get separated from me," he said. "Our hosts would not understand you anyway, if you were to stray too far." He did not say the word "darkenwraiths" or mention their mission in front of the others, and he had given Julia strict orders to do likewise.

Last of all, Pallantu instructed Julia to say some encouraging words to him. She didn't dare to ask if she could try making him weaker. But it probably wouldn't work on such a powerful creator anyway.

Between rounds of training with her talent, Julia received short lectures about the darkenwraiths – about their nature (which was mysterious), their weaknesses (which were few), their strengths and how they tended to behave.

At last, when the day's lesson was complete, Pallantu sent her home to the Academy with a final, fateful command: "Tell your little brother that we leave immediately after breakfast."

"But why does he even have to know that I'm going?" asked Julia. "If it's supposed to go as quickly as you say?"

"He needs to know," Pallantu said, "because he is coming with us."

Julia gasped. "No! Not Edvin! He's only ten!"

"And he is one of the few people to ever best Korak in battle," Pallantu pointed out. "And it is likely that he is one of two who can open your father's special locks."

"But, but …" Julia stammered. A thought dawned on her, and it came as a relief. "But what if he doesn't *want* to come along? We can't force him!"

Pallantu considered. "True. But if half of what I have heard about him and all that I know about you and your father is true, then he will not hesitate. Which is good, because it will be much easier for us if he is with us. It will also be much easier to send you both home."

"Easier to send us home? What do you mean?"

Pallantu hesitated. "I did not want to burden you with this knowledge," he said at last. "But it seems I have no choice but to tell you."

"Tell me what?"

"This expedition is also my plan to return you to your world. It will be much easier if we leave from Sulallia rather than this domain."

"Why? We got here easily enough. With Lars-Petter's help, of course, but …"

"The Council do not want you to leave the city."

Julia stared. "What? Why not?"

Pallantu sighed. "Well, now that I have told you part of it, I suppose I must tell you all of it. There are certain councilmembers who are troubled by the fact that Korak was pursuing you. They fear he may use you to open the chest himself, and they suspect he may have other reasons for wanting to capture you. They want to know what those reasons are before they let you go. Though they are probably never going to find out. Which means …"

"We're prisoners here," Julia realised.

"I am afraid so," said Pallantu. "But I plan to set you free, to send you home as soon as we have recovered the Darkenstar. But I doubt I would get the chance to smuggle you out twice. So you shall both have to accompany me to Sulallia, now, when the Council is not expecting it. From there it will be much easier to send you home. Edvin may of course choose to stay here and wait for us, and in that case I shall do my best to send him home afterwards. But I fear that it may take a very long time. Your mother would likely miss him."

Julia shuddered. "She probably misses us already. No, let's just do this and get home as soon as possible. But …" She hesitated. "If Edvin comes with us, can you promise he'll be safe?"

Pallantu smiled and gestured expansively. "I am Pallantor's safety," he said. "If he stays close to me, then he shall be as safe as if he were hidden in this very tower."

Julia was forced to wake Edvin and tell him everything as soon as Pallantu's guard had escorted her home to the Academy. She couldn't go to sleep with the heavy conversation hanging over her.

But to her surprise, the conversation wasn't nearly as difficult as she had feared. "So we get to save the world!" Edvin interrupted as soon as he had understood her cautious explanation.

"I don't think you understand," she said. "We're going to Sulallia. Where Korak lives."

"Korak who I've already beaten once," Edvin pointed out. "We're going to be heroes! Just like Dad!"

Julia didn't know how she was supposed to answer. "This isn't a game, Edvin," she said at last. "It's really dangerous. Deadly dangerous! You beat part of Korak before, but now we're going to meet him for real."

"And beat him for real," he said. "Imagine if we can

do more than just save our world and this one. What if we can save Kasir's world too? So that he can go home. Do you think we can?"

"Well … Pallantu didn't say anything about that," said Julia. "He just said that we were supposed to get the Darkenstar and that he would send us home."

"But we have to save Kasir's world!" said Edvin.

Julia considered giving Edvin a proper lecture about how serious this was, but then she changed her mind. After all, she wanted him to come along so they could get home as soon as possible. And besides, she knew her words had power. Maybe it was her earlier encouragement that had made him so self-confident now. What if she made an effort to scare him, and it made him so frightened and weak that he couldn't handle travelling to Sulallia? Better that he be strong and brave. And it would probably also be better for them to be a bit quiet. After all, Kasir lay sleeping in the next room.

"We'll have to do exactly as Pallantu says," she said quietly. "He knows what's best in the long run. Maybe the Darkenstar can help him and the Council to save Kasir's world later, even if we don't manage to do everything tomorrow. It might take time to save a whole world."

Edvin crossed his arms and sighed. "Maybe," he said. "But didn't Maja say that the worlds here in Thousandworld were pretty small? She called them domains. Maybe a little domain doesn't take quite as much time to save as a whole, big world. Anyway, should we go wake Kasir and tell him?"

233

Julia stared at her brother in disbelief. "Haven't you understood a word of what I've said? We can't tell anyone! If the Council found out about Pallantu's plan, then they could stop us, and we'd never get home!"

"But Kasir is our friend," Edvin protested. "Are we really going to disappear without saying good-bye or telling him where we're going? He's going to miss us and think something's happened to us – and he's going to be so lonely."

"Lonely?" Julia snorted. "He's a prince here. Everyone loves Kasir."

"Yes," said Edvin. "But he doesn't have any friends, no one he can hang out with. Just us."

Julia realised that Edvin was right. Despite all the bowing and respectful whistling, despite the fact that Kasir seemed to be able to do as he pleased, she had never seen him just *hang out* with anyone – except for her and Edvin. She thought about what he had said in the park. *Zero friend.* Could it really be true that he had no friends?

"We can each write a letter to him," she said at last. "We can stick the letters under his door after breakfast tomorrow, right before we leave. But we should write quickly and get it over with, and then we need to sleep. It's already late, and we have a long day ahead of us."

Edvin snorted. "You sound just like Mum," he said. "That's exactly what she would say if she were here."

"And she'd be right," said Julia. "But go on and write your letter – short and quick. Get as much sleep as you can."

Despite her words, she took a long time writing her own letter. As she sat at the desk in her room and wrote, it occurred to her that this letter could be the last that Kasir ever heard from her. What did she really want to say to him? She was almost thankful when she heard a door open out in the corridor. Maybe Edvin was coming to ask her how to spell something. Julia went to the door, ready for his knock. When it didn't come, she opened the door a crack and looked out, but she didn't see anyone in the empty corridor. Then she shook her head, went back to her desk and began to write. The first letter she wrote felt very formal, almost devoid of feelings. Her second try turned out far too emotional. She didn't want Kasir to think that she *liked* him or anything!

Julia's third try wasn't much of a success either, but it was going to have to do. It was late now, and she was starting to yawn. She changed into the long, white nightshirt that Maja had packed for her and lay down in the soft bed.

Although she was exhausted, her anxious thoughts made it hard for her to fall sleep, and when she had finally succeeded, she dreamed strange dreams and woke several times. Once she was awakened by a door opening and closing out in the corridor. Was it Edvin, coming to tell her about nightmares of his own? But he never came to her door, and at last she turned over and went back to sleep.

26

Julia didn't see Kasir at breakfast the next morning. She found herself surprised at how much his absence saddened her; she had really wanted to at least see his face one more time.

It was obvious that Edvin was eager to tell his friends from martial arts all about his great, exciting mission. But he couldn't, and he couldn't say goodbye to them either. As they ate, she saw how he grew more and more despondent.

"You can at least say thank you," she said at last. "Say it from both of us if you can. They're not going to understand why, but it will be good to say it."

Edvin whistled something to the boys, and they looked at him strangely. Hullevin, who had been the first to welcome Julia to the table, answered something incomprehensible in Sulallian. Julia smiled at him sadly. *I'm going to miss him*, she realised.

Over Hullevin's shoulder, she caught sight of the back of Lalora's head with its three black braids. Maybe it was just as well she had failed to make the girl weak, she thought reluctantly. She was, after all, training to fight against the darkenwraiths. But at least she would never be able to torment Edvin again.

When they had eaten, they went upstairs to their rooms, gathered their belongings and slid their letters in through the crack under Kasir's door. They didn't have a lot of belongings to gather. Pallantu had told them not to take anything with them. Julia had nevertheless insisted that they should each pack a small bag with a change of clothes and a water bottle, in addition to the mirror and the dagger.

With her pack slung over her shoulder, she hurried down to the room with all the desks. There she chose a paper full of drawings from her competition with Kasir – they had all stopped moving long ago, but still, it was a nice memory. To her disappointment, she did not find Kasir at his desk. Strangely enough, the repaired lute was nowhere to be found, either.

Doneus sat at his new desk. Julia managed to wave to him, blush and hope that a wave didn't mean anything bad in this world. Then she hurried to the main entrance where Edvin stood waiting for her.

Pallantu's guard was supposed to meet them by a statue some distance away from the Academy. Pallantu wanted to avoid any suspicions that might arise if the man were seen fetching both of them at once.

The streets were crowded, but Julia recognised the hulking guard standing in the shadow of a statue, despite the fact that the man was now dressed in a hooded white robe and carried a walking stick instead of a poleaxe.

When the guard saw them, he said something brief in Sulallian and nodded. To Julia's surprise, Edvin whistled something in reply. "He's telling us to follow him," he explained.

"Well of course we're supposed to follow him," said Julia. "Do you really think I didn't understand that?" And so they followed the huge man's white-clad back through the crowd.

Soon they turned aside from the crowded street, to a deserted alley leading into a quieter neighbourhood. It was then that Julia noticed Kasir.

First she heard his footsteps behind them – quick, even footsteps on the cobblestones, light but not sneaking. Then she turned and saw him, dressed all in white aside from a peculiar black belt around his waist. The belt was heavily laden with brushes and bulging pockets, and the young prince had a simple backpack slung over one shoulder.

"Kasir?" Julia said, surprised.

"Kasir!" Edvin cheered. He rushed to greet the young prince. "I thought …"

He was interrupted by a stern exclamation from Pallantu's guard. Julia didn't understand what the huge man said, but his voice was like thunder, angry and frightening. His gaze was terrible.

Kasir stood with his head held high, glaring back at the man. He pronounced a few Sulallian words with a mixture of anger and a prince's self-evident expectation to be obeyed.

The guard answered and took a step closer to Kasir. "What are they saying?" Julia whispered. But Edvin was silent, staring in horror at the huge man.

The guard raised his walking stick threateningly.

In a flash, Kasir had a brush in his hand. The guard cried out as the staff was knocked out of his hands by a grey streak that the boy painted in the air. He roared and threw himself at Kasir, but the young prince just stepped to one side and waved his brush, and the man landed heavily on the cobblestones, bound hand and foot with coils of grey. He roared something, and Kasir covered his mouth with grey.

"Come," he said, continuing along the alley as the helpless guard struggled on the white cobblestones.

Julia ran after Kasir. "What have you done?" she said, horrified. "Why?"

Edvin was quick to defend his friend. "It was self-defence, Julia!" he said. "He would have hit him with that stick!"

"But he's Pallantu's guard!" she said. "Kasir, you can't just … And he was supposed to show us the way!"

"Way easy," said Kasir. "Pallantu. I … feel. Pallantu big crator. Strong. I feel crator. Mum teach me."

"You can feel where creators are?" Edvin said, impressed. "Cool!"

"But how did you know we're going to meet Pallantu?" Julia asked. "And why are you here at all?"

"I come with," said Kasir. "Sulallia. My home."

Julia suddenly remembered the door that had opened in the middle of the night. She gave Edvin a suspicious glance. "You told him, didn't you? Even though I said it was secret!"

Edvin shook his head vigorously. "No, Julia, it wasn't me, I promise."

Kasir laughed. "Edvin told, Julia told. Secret quiet. You not quiet. Room close."

"You heard us," said Julia. "I thought you were sleeping! I knew we should have been quieter. But anyway, you can't come with us. Pallantu said it was only supposed to be us three. This is very important – more important than you can understand!"

"Pallantu not decide," said Kasir.

"But Kasir," she said. "He's the leader of the Council. He's the greatest creator in this world, and he has a very important plan. I don't know if you heard everything we said, but his plan can save our world, this world – maybe your world too."

Kasir snorted. "Pallantu not greatest crator," he said, pointing skyward for some reason that Julia couldn't understand. "And Pallantu not prince Sulallia," he added, with emphasis. His gaze hardened.

"Kasir," said Julia. "You can't just attack the bodyguard of the most important man in the city and leave him in an alley. That must be illegal! Don't you have to hide or something now? What do you think Pallantu will do when he hears what you've done?"

Kasir didn't answer.

240

"But he didn't hurt him," Edvin pointed out. "And anyway, it was self-defence. Besides, maybe we don't have to tell Pallantu."

Kasir led them through a garden, over a small bridge across a stream, and into another part of the city. As they walked, Edvin babbled on and on, but Kasir was ominously quiet, and Julia was lost in her own thoughts about what she would say when they reached Pallantu. He was sure to ask what had happened to his guard. And why Julia hadn't kept everything secret as she had promised.

At last Kasir came to a sudden halt at a crossroads of deserted alleys. Julia and Edvin also stopped, looking around in confusion.

"Well, Pallantu?" said Kasir. "Do you intend to show yourself? I know you're here, speaker."

"Kasir!" Edvin gasped. "Your accent is gone! You can speak Swedish now!"

"Or perhaps it is you who can speak Sulallian," Pallantu said, appearing out of thin air in front of Kasir. He adjusted one of his rings. "You saw me, Your Highness – impressive. Perhaps I shall have to speak to Galena about this ring. And I see you." He spoke in a normal conversational tone, and the gaze he fixed on the young prince was as dispassionate as marble. Still, Julia got the impression that his words contained some subtle threat.

"I will accompany you to Sulallia," Kasir said, meeting the man's gaze.

Pallantu sighed. "Your Highness, I had hoped to spare you what we are about to see. Sulallia is no longer the Sulallia you remember."

"Yet it is still *my* Sulallia, Pallantu."

"I understand your zeal for your domain, Your Highness. It is only natural to feel a certain responsibility for one's domain. I know well what a burden it can be to lead a domain in war and to bear the responsibility of caring for one's people – for several peoples, as well as a number of regents." He gave Kasir a significant look.

"You have no responsibility for me, Pallantu."

Pallantu looked hurt. "Your Highness, you forget the decision of the Council! We are on your side. One day, when it is possible, we will win back Sulallia for you and your people. And until that day, I will be your guardian and keep you safe. Which means, among other things, keeping you away from the darkenwraiths until you are ready."

"I am ready now, speaker," Kasir said coldly. "And with regards to the Council's decision that you should be my guardian …"

"Choose your words carefully, Your Highness," Pallantu interrupted. "Words have great power. What is said cannot be unsaid, and more than three thousand of your people are entirely dependent on the walls of Pallantor for their safety."

Kasir's eyes blazed. "Mr Speaker," he said after a long silence. "I intend to travel to Sulallia today, with or without you. You cannot keep me here against my will. The three thousand that you mentioned would hardly be pleased to hear that their prince was being held captive."

Pallantu sighed deeply. "I suppose it is not possible to make you see reason, Your Highness. Much like last time. Perhaps I should be thankful that you at least deign to speak with me this time, rather than just sneaking out of the city without a word. You cannot imagine how much unrest you caused by disappearing without informing anyone last time."

"Those who needed to know were informed," said Kasir.

Julia saw how Pallantu's hands clenched and his mouth narrowed to a thin white line. But instead of answering, he simply gave a slight bow. Then he turned to Julia and Edvin.

"Well," he said, "we were supposed to be four, and we are four. I suppose my bodyguard found something else to occupy him?" He didn't look at Kasir, and he didn't wait for an answer. "Perhaps that is just as well. Maintaining invisibility for five people would be quite taxing."

"Are we going to be invisible?" Edvin said, mouth agape.

Pallantu's lips curled in a brief hint of a smile. "If you stay close to me and do exactly as I say, yes. This is the plan. We proceed to the portal, invisible to everyone here. Then we carry on straight to the throne room, invisible to all the darkenwraiths. Regardless of what you see or hear, stay close to me, and keep moving. If you must speak, do it quietly. It could be too taxing for me to conceal both the sight and the sound of us at the same time. When we have reached the throne room, Julia is to open the chest. Then we return to Sulallia's portal yard, I send Edvin and Julia to their home world, and His Highness and I return to Pallantor. Do you have any questions?"

"Yes," said Edvin. "What do we do if we see Korak? Should I fight him like last time?"

Pallantu's gaze fell on the boy, his eyes as hard as sapphires. "It is probably for the best that I make this clear to you now, Edvin. You drove off a shadow of a shadow of Korak, in a domain where the darkenwraiths do not reign. An impressive feat, but now we are going to a domain which is firmly under their control. If we should happen to meet the real Korak at his full power, then you are to stay close to me and do exactly as I say. I will see to it that he does not notice any of us, and we will pass by him and take what we have come for."

"But what if we're seen?" Edvin argued. "Kasir saw you, didn't he?"

Pallantu grimaced. "That is another matter entirely. We shall have to hope that the darkenwraiths do not have any overly talented princes who do things that should not be possible. But regardless of what happens, stay close to me. Come." He beckoned them closer.

Julia stepped forward, and Pallantu raised his hands and began to chant a poem over them. Unlike all other speech in his presence, the poem was incomprehensible. Or rather, Julia could not make out any words, but the rhythmic sounds filled her mind with impressions: a cool breeze, darkness and an expansive desert, flat and barren all the way to the horizon.

"No one will see us now," said Pallantu. "Stay close to me, and we shall proceed to the portal." He turned and led them further along the alley.

Julia followed with Edvin on one side and Kasir on the other. As they walked, she took Edvin's hand and held it, just like she had done when they were younger and had to cross the road. She didn't know why she did it – maybe an instinctive feeling that the closer together they stayed, the more invisible they would be. She almost expected him to shake off her hand. After all, he was ten years old now. But instead, he squeezed her hand, and she squeezed back.

Kasir looked as if he was lost in thought. Julia really wanted to speak to him. Hearing him speak clearly and correctly made such a difference. He sounded more intelligent, more confident, less like a frightened refugee boy and more like a mighty prince. And now, in Pallantu's presence, he would have the words to tell her about anything. To explain how it was that he had appeared in Klippsby several months ago. Or to describe his world. Though of course, she was about to see it for herself.

After a long walk through the city, they arrived at a green park with sculptures made of various kinds of metal and stone. Pallantu led them to a large bronze sculpture of a hand holding a lantern. There was text on the sculpture's base, and as Pallantu laid his hands on the great hand and chanted quietly, Julia read it. "The light shines in the darkness, and the darkness has not overcome it."

"It's in Swedish," Edvin pointed out.

"No," said Julia. "Pallantu's power makes it so that we can read it."

Pallantu looked up from the sculpture. "Your brother is right. The artist who created this portal came from your world. But allow me to focus."

Edvin gave Julia a triumphant look, and she rolled her eyes. Then the park disappeared around them.

27

Sulallia was not what Julia had expected – not like the dark, frightening forest in Maja's world or the ominous, abandoned garden city in Paradisum. In fact, it was much, much worse.

There was no sun to be seen, but the dark sky was a bit lighter towards the horizon, as if dawn were on its way. In the dim light, Julia saw the silhouettes of various sculptures crowding the overgrown grassy area where they now stood. Beyond the sculptures, a landscape of rolling hills stretched out to the horizon. Julia saw small groves of dark trees, a distant lake, a stream and some stone buildings in the middle distance. It should have been beautiful, just as the sculptures should have been beautiful – but everything looked wrong. After a moment, she realised what it was. The shadows. They weren't behaving as they should. Long shadows spread out on the grass in all directions. Certain sculptures had shadows on the wrong side or on several sides. Some of the shadows moved, but not in time with each other or with the slight breeze.

Julia suddenly realised what she was seeing, and her blood froze. She backed closer to Pallantu and pulled her little brother with her. They backed into Kasir, and she turned and saw that he was looking in an entirely different direction, towards a large palace with five towers. The building seemed to have been ravaged by a great fire, and one of the towers had partially crumbled. Smoke hovered in the air over the palace – but just as the shadows were no ordinary shadows, it was no ordinary smoke.

Something moved in the corner of Julia's eye, and Edvin cried out. Julia turned just in time to see a lanky figure like a living shadow disappear behind a statue.

"Keep quiet," Pallantu hissed. "Or at least warn me if you intend to shriek like that. I barely had time to cover the sound."

"B-but, I s-saw," Edvin stammered. He held his silver dagger in a white-knuckled grip. Julia drew the hand mirror from her pocket. Even if she didn't know what she would do with it, it felt good to have something in her hand, something to strike with if the darkenwraiths came too close.

"They cannot see us," said Pallantu. "We are completely invisible, as long as you stay close to me and keep quiet."

"All right," Edvin said hesitantly. "Sorry."

Pallantu turned to Julia. "Could you please speak some courage into your brother?" he said. "It could save our lives. But come, follow me." He led them off towards the palace.

As they walked, Julia squeezed Edvin's hand and whispered to him. She said that he was strong and brave, reminded him of how he had fought Korak before and saved her life. But the words felt hollow here, as they walked through such terrible darkness. It was as if the ground had been defiled by the darkenwraiths. Long, flat shadows without any apparent source swept slowly over the ground like the tentacles of some colossal squid. One of these enormous, shadowy tentacles curled lazily towards them and passed under their feet. Julia shivered and squeezed Edvin's hand and the handle of the mirror. As the shadow passed, she heard a voice like wind whispering in distant treetops: *grave dirt.* Then the tentacle was past.

When it swept under them again, Kasir spat on it. Pallantu groaned. "Your Highness, could you please show some restraint?"

"I cannot stand its boasting," Kasir said, not the slightest bit apologetic.

They continued onward through the remains of a large garden. It must have been indescribably beautiful once, with its bushes and bridges, sculptures and ponds. But now it was eerie. Here too, the shadows lay at strange angles, and some of them moved. The entire place had been wrecked by the darkness.

"My mother's well," Kasir said softly, pointing to a small, pretty stone well in the shade of a tree. "It was a wedding present from my father. He dug it and built it with his own hands. My mother used to stand here and paint. Sometimes she simply stood looking down into its depths. She said she could see the Great Creator's beauty down there. This was where she found inspiration. What if …?" He took a step towards the well.

"Wait!" Pallantu hissed, seizing his arm. "Your Highness! Do not look. It is in exactly such places that our enemy loves to set his most dangerous traps."

Kasir stopped in his tracks. He heaved a great sigh. "Would you stop me from looking into my mother's well, Pallantu? But perhaps you are right. It's hard to know if …"

He fell silent as a beautiful woman with long, black hair appeared by the well. Her dark eyes peered down into its depths. "Remember," she whispered in a voice like a distant echo on the breeze. "Remember who you are."

"Mother?" Kasir took a step forward, but the woman did not appear to see or hear him.

At that moment, a dark tentacle rose from the ground and passed through her, and she vanished in a puff of smoke.

Kasir roared, drew two brushes from his belt and hurled long grey brushstrokes at the tentacle. Then he lunged at it, stabbing with his brushes. The long, snakelike shadow let out a shriek and tried to slither away, but Kasir nailed it to the ground with a brush and stabbed it several times in rapid succession with the other.

Pallantu swore.

Suddenly, it was as if all the darkness in the garden woke to life and attacked them. Julia screamed as several dark coils rose around her and Edvin. She struck with the mirror as Edvin stabbed with the silver dagger, and they were rewarded with otherworldly shrieks. Here in Pallantu's presence, the darkenwraiths' cries formed words: *Pain! Death! Take! Avenge! Devour! Darken! Destroy!*

Meanwhile, Kasir was painting desperately in the air. Light grey birds and butterflies went after the dark creatures. Thick brushstrokes flew as Kasir leaped out of the way of long, dark arms.

Pallantu stood drawing signs in the air with his fingers as he chanted a poem about thunder and fire. The darkenwraiths around him burst into flame and disappeared. But one was too quick. A black, eyeless head came roaring towards Pallantu and sunk its shadowy teeth into his wrist. He cried out in pain before setting the creature on fire and throwing it away.

"Run!" he cried, fleeing towards the palace. "Run!"

Julia pulled Edvin along, and the three children ran after the tall, white-clad man. Pallantu cleared a path for them with burning symbols drawn in the air as he chanted a poem about forgetfulness and the darkness beyond the stars. When they had arrived at the moat around the palace, he suddenly stopped short, and Julia almost ran into him. She turned around with her mirror raised, but their pursuers were nowhere to be seen.

"You must obey me!" Pallantu growled. Julia was not sure if he meant all three of them or just Kasir, who he was glaring at. "We must stay together and keep quiet. No more outcries. No more foolish attacks on the darkenwraiths."

"But it was Kasir's mum," Edvin said lamely.

"No," said Pallantu, "It was an illusion, created by the darkenwraiths. Do not believe anything you see here. Do not believe anything you hear. Believe me, and me alone. Trust me, obey me, and we will take the Darkenstar and escape with our lives."

Kasir made no answer, but he sniffled a bit. Julia wished she could comfort him but didn't know what she was supposed to say. To see the image of his mother, alive again, and then to see how the darkenwraith destroyed it – it must have been indescribably terrible. She would probably have reacted in exactly the same way.

"Now then," said Pallantu. "We are standing on the wrong side of the palace. If we are fortunate, the drawbridge will be down. Otherwise, I shall take care of it. Stay close to me, and obey!" He turned around, and then Julia caught sight of his left hand, which the darkenwraith had bitten. It was completely black.

"Pallantu," she said. "Your hand – are you all right?"

He looked at the black hand and licked his lips. "I will be perfectly fine soon enough," he said. "But we must be quick. No more questions. Let me focus."

He led them around the dark moat, whispering poetry as he walked.

Edvin gasped. Julia followed his gaze and saw something large and dark moving in the depths. "Don't look," she whispered. "They can't see us. You don't need to be afraid – remember, you're strong and brave! You were wonderful against those darkenwraiths in the park."

"Thanks," Edvin said weakly. "But I felt so scared that I didn't even know what I was doing."

"Me neither," Julia admitted. "But we won. You made it. And you're going to keep making it. Remember that you're holding Dad's dagger, and he was a great creator and a hero."

Edvin's hand found hers and squeezed it in the darkness.

At last they arrived at the gate on the far side of the moat. Thankfully, the drawbridge was down and lay like a bridge over the water. But the dark figures standing on the drawbridge made Julia gasp.

Half a dozen pitch-black soldiers with three-horned heads stood at attention in two rows along the drawbridge, guarding it. Each soldier stood straight-backed, with both hands resting on the pommel of a long, black sword, the dark point of which rested on the drawbridge's shadow-stained wood.

"They cannot see us," Pallantu whispered. "Stay close to me and keep quiet."

As they approached the shadow soldiers, Julia began to hear their voices, like deep echoes in underground caves. Their speech was like Pallantu's poems

– complex and mighty, and almost completely incomprehensible, though Julia got a sense of a word or phrase now and then. *Light is darkness. Might is freedom. Decay. Eternity. Loneliness is greatness. All is nothing.*

Edvin squeezed her hand hard as they passed between the motionless guards. Close up, their horrible speech filled the air so that Julia felt as if she would suffocate. She wanted to flee or to scream, to knock their dark words away with her hands or give in to them, let the dark speech fill her, make her powerful and free and …

Then they arrived at the other side of the drawbridge and she shook her head. Seized by a sudden impulse, she looked into the mirror, perhaps to see if the darkenwraiths' words had left her ears as dirty as they felt. Really, she should hardly have been able to see anything in that darkness as they passed through the opening in the thick castle wall. But somehow, she caught a glimpse of herself. What she saw could hardly be expressed in words – but it was better than the soldiers' dark promises. When she lowered the mirror again, the effect of their speech was gone.

She squeezed Edvin's hand. "You made it."

They came out on the other side of the wall, into a broad courtyard surrounding the palace proper. Enormous shadowy shapes lay resting in the grass – creatures as large as the flying monsters they had seen in the desert outside Maja's valley. Julia's stomach dropped when she saw them. *They can't see us*, she reminded herself. *They can't see us.*

Nonetheless, she walked on tip-toe after Pallantu, hardly daring to breathe.

They crossed the courtyard and climbed up a broad stone staircase, finally arriving at a pair of enormous, closed double doors. Pallantu tried the handles, but the doors were locked.

His poems ceased. He laid a hand on the crack between the two doors, and in a loud, commanding voice, said, "Open!"

The power of his voice vibrated through Julia's entire body. But the doors did not budge. However, one of the enormous black creatures behind them lifted its head.

28

Pallantu rushed to the waking darkenwraith's side and hastily began writing on its flank with his fingertips. The creature's enormous, triangular head sank slowly as glowing symbols appeared on its black body.

Edvin tugged at Julia's hand. "Come on!" he said. "We have to stay close to him."

Right. They might be completely visible where they stood! Julia and Edvin hurried to Pallantu's side, and thankfully, Kasir came with them.

When they had arrived, the enormous monster lay motionless on the grass, and the glowing symbols slowly faded out.

Pallantu panted, wiping sweat from his brow. "I cannot imagine why your father would have such a defence on the door," he said to Kasir, irritated. "Were you expecting a visit from some unwelcome wordcrafter?"

"My father was a very wise man," said Kasir. "But I believe the door was my mother's idea. Sometimes she was even wiser than my father."

Pallantu laughed bitterly. "No matter. I know more than wordcraft." He adjusted some of the rings on his fingers and approached the door again.

"Wait," said Kasir. "I believe that I can open the door. If you turn towards the darkenwraiths and continue to speak invisibility over us, I should be able to do it."

"I do not need to look at them to speak invisibility," Pallantu pointed out.

"Begging your pardon, Mr Speaker," said Kasir. "But this is Sulallian custom. It would not do for Sulallia's prince to reveal the door's secret to a foreign leader."

"Not even a foreign leader who is your guardian? This knowledge could be important for your domain's future, Your Highness."

"Not as important as the future regent's ability to keep his word. Turn around if you please, Mr Speaker."

Pallantu's voice sounded darker and deeper than normal as he began to chant invisibility over them again. But he turned around.

"Should we look away too?" Edvin asked. But Kasir shook his head.

The young prince placed one hand on a sun carved among the curling patterns on the door, and the other hand on a moon. Then he bowed his head and pressed his lips against a carved flower.

The doors swung slowly inward.

Pallantu whirled to face them, but Kasir was already on his feet again. The young prince drew a brush and painted a small glowing ball, which he held in his hand as he led them onward. "The throne room is this way," he said.

The palace was large, and the wide stone corridors were decorated with tapestries, suits of armour standing in alcoves, and here and there a sculpture rising up in the middle of the floor. It probably would have been beautiful in the daylight, but in the dim bubble of light from Kasir's glowing ball, with shadows shifting around them as they walked, it was unsettling. Julia felt as if something in the darkness was looking right at her, despite Pallantu's invisibility.

After a while, they heard the sound of pouring water. They arrived at an intersection of two corridors and encountered a woman in a long dress, pouring water from a vase into a round basin. It took Julia a moment to realise that the woman was a statue. A fountain.

"The water from the fountain is meant to give strength and joy," Kasir said quietly as they approached.

"I implore you, Your Highness," said Pallantu. "Do not drink. Think of what happened at the well – our enemy is exceptionally skilled at setting such traps."

Kasir shrugged and passed by the fountain without a backward glance.

They climbed a long staircase to the next level – and a dark figure came floating past them in the corridor at the top, nearly crashing into Kasir. The young prince stumbled and almost fell down the stairs, but Julia caught him.

"Thank you," he said, shaken.

The entire floor turned out to be full of the floating black figures. They were approximately human-shaped, but lacked clear arms or legs. Each time one glided past, Julia heard the same word, like a whisper on the breeze, over and over again: *power*. She shuddered.

These darkenwraiths flew at great speeds, and Julia and the others were forced to duck out of the way several times to avoid colliding with them. Julia didn't want to think what might happen if she touched one.

Thankfully, the darkenwraiths only flew in one direction – toward them from the front. Julia imagined the creatures must be flying around and around in a great circle, chanting *power, power, power* … but why?

Julia and her companions left the corridor and stepped out into an enormous chamber lit by the dark blue sky outside the high windows. Directly below the windows, perhaps fifteen metres over their heads, an exquisitely crafted balcony ran the length of the room. A broad marble staircase led up to the balcony, and at the top of the stairs was a pair of huge, closed double doors.

The entire chamber was ominously empty. Julia didn't even see any strange shadows. At the entrance of the room, the four of them stopped. The only sound to be heard was Pallantu's poetry about invisibility and silence, which echoed disconcertingly from the high walls. Then, at last, he fell silent.

"The throne room lies behind those doors," he said, pointing up the stairs. "There we will find the chest containing the Darkenstar. There our enemy's full attention is focused. Stay close to me – hold a corner of my mantle. Say nothing, and walk lightly. No matter what you see, do not be frightened, do not cry out, do not run. Follow me calmly and silently, and I will protect you. I will lead you to the chest, and Julia will open it. Otherwise Edvin will. Then I will take the Darkenstar, and we will leave calmly and quietly. Is that understood?"

They nodded, and Pallantu began chanting again and led them across the echoing hall and up the steps. Outside the double doors, he paused to give them one last warning. "Do not believe anything you see or hear in there. Listen to me, and me alone."

Then he resumed his recitation and pushed one of the heavy doors. It swung open with a loud creak.

The throne room was a large, five-sided room, lighter than the great chamber outside, as there were huge windows in all the walls except the one through which they had entered. The ceiling was high, and the floor was a mosaic of stone tiles. In the middle of the floor stood five statues in a ring – human figures busy with various forms of art. No darkenwraiths were to be seen. The only really dark place in the room was a pitch black corner behind a raised platform where two elegant, golden thrones stood. Pallantu led them carefully towards this platform as he spoke invisibility over them.

As they approached the sculptures, Julia recognised one of the five – a tall man holding a harp. *Lars-Petter!* And the man who stood beside him, with a long pair of tongs in one hand and a ring in the other, could it be …?

"Dad," Edvin breathed. Julia shushed him. But she had a difficult time tearing her gaze from the statue as Pallantu led them onward. So it was not until they had reached the low steps leading up to the platform that she discovered that the darkness behind the two thrones was moving. She shrank back in fear.

"You can stop with your poetry now," a deep voice thundered, seeming to come from every direction at once. "I see you."

The door behind them crashed shut. Julia turned and discovered to her horror that both doors had gone completely black.

Pallantu fell silent. Julia turned back to the platform and watched as the darkness behind the thrones rose, taking the shape of a towering figure with oily, smoke-like tentacles of shadow.

"Welcome," said Korak. "I have been waiting for you for quite some time."

29

"Korak," Pallantu said in a confident, commanding voice. "I know your name, but you do not know mine. You know the advantage this gives me. I know you can feel the combined power that I and my companions possess. Leave this chamber now, and you may keep your poor parody of a life for a little while longer."

The dark figure chuckled. "Do you really believe that you can fool me with all your lies? You don't understand as much as you think – not about me, not about us, not about what you call the Darkenstar. Haven't you realised what I can do with its power, *Pallantu Alaravin?*"

Pallantu cleared his throat. "You and I both know that you do not have the Darkenstar yet. Depart from this chamber now or be destroyed. We have the power to completely annihilate you here and now."

"And do you really think that would make any difference?" Korak said. His deep voice dripped with disdain. "No, Pallantu – there is much that you do not understand – not even about yourself." He slid towards them threateningly, growing as he approached.

Julia and Edvin inched closer to Pallantu, who backed away a step. The room began to feel heavier, darker, more closed in. Julia glanced behind her and saw several dark creatures with tentacles taking shape by the walls. She screamed. They were surrounded by Korak's shadows!

Pallantu raised his hands and chanted a fateful poem about fire and destruction. Then he hurled a billow of flame at Korak, who suddenly grew to double his previous size and raised a forest of tentacles to counterattack.

Meanwhile, Kasir threw nets and birds and grey brushstrokes at Korak's shadows, with no visible effect.

Edvin let go of Julia's hand, and with a shout, he threw himself at one of the shadows with his dagger raised to strike. Julia wanted to run after him but stood as if frozen. What could she do, really? Without any weapons or even anywhere to run? She raised her hands reflexively to shield herself, wishing that she could wake up and find that this was all just a terrible dream.

Then she caught sight of her reflection in the silver hand mirror. The Julia she saw was neither helpless nor weaponless, but a creator, Henrik Andersson's daughter. She had her creator talent and one of Henrik Andersson's magical creations – and she also had a little brother to protect. She ran after Edvin, who stood with his dagger held out in front of him as one of the shadows circled him warily, hissing threats.

"Don't listen to it, Edvin!" she said. "You're strong! You're fast! Your dagger is powerful! And you've already beaten him once!"

Her words seemed to encourage Edvin, and he threw himself at the shadow with his dagger raised to strike. Dark tentacles shot out and pulled him into a deadly embrace, but the darkenwraith cried out as Edvin thrust his dagger into its belly.

Meanwhile, another darkenwraith pounced on Julia. She struck at its shapeless head with the hand mirror, but the head drew back on a long, flexible neck, and dark tentacles wrapped around her. The creature laughed, and Julia felt a familiar chill deep in her bones – the same cold she had felt when the flying darkenwraith had attacked her on the way to Pallantor.

"Do you really believe that you can stand against me?" the darkenwraith laughed, pulling her down to the floor. Julia felt herself grow weak. It felt as if she were falling endlessly, faster and faster.

The dark face filled her field of vision. "Soon you will be one of us," said the darkenwraith. "Imagine – Henrik Andersson's daughter, our tool. Imagine what wondrous art we will be able to create through you!"

Julia's arms felt distant, as if they belonged to someone else's body. Nevertheless she summoned up the last of her strength and struck with the mirror.

The reflective side hit the darkenwraith's head, and the creature let out a blood-curdling screech and fled toward the wall, scuttling like a monstrous spider.

Edvin, who had just defeated his opponent, thrust the point of the dagger into it, and it writhed for a moment and then vanished. He rushed to Julia's side. "Are you all right?"

"I'm … I … I'll be fine," Julia said, rising unsteadily to her feet. She looked at the mirror in wonder. Did it really have such power? In her reflection, she sensed a hint of an answer: *Yes, I do – and you do too.* She stood up straight. "I'm fine," she said. "Come on – we have to help Kasir!"

The young prince stood surrounded by three shadows. He backed slowly towards the wall as they fought through his nets.

"You can do this, Kasir!" Julia shouted. "You're a powerful creator! Remember how you fixed the lute!"

Suddenly one of the light grey nets caught one of the darkenwraiths, who fell, bound, with a violent hissing. Edvin pounced on it and destroyed it with his dagger.

A thump and a groan caught Julia's attention, and she whirled around to find that Pallantu had been thrown against the wall and was sliding limply to the floor. Korak came gliding towards him, huge and dark and horrible. "Is this the best you can do, Pallantu?" he asked derisively.

"Of course he can do better!" Julia shouted. "He's Pallantor's mightiest creator! He has lots of power and even more knowledge! He's studied for years to become an expert in defeating you!"

Korak turned his head and regarded her with an eyeless face. "How little you know, girl," he said. "You haven't understood who you're following, or what he—"

A cascade of blue light from Pallantu's hands caught him in the side, and he was hurled away, shrieking.

"The chest!" Pallantu panted, leaping to his feet and pursuing the darkenwraith. "Get to the chest!"

Julia turned towards the platform. Behind the two thrones, where Korak had previously brooded as a shapeless black mass, stood a fine chest made of dark, polished wood, with beautiful silver and gold inlay. She ran towards it.

A shadowy tentacle grabbed her foot and tripped her. She hit the ground hard and swung desperately with the mirror. An icy chill crept up her leg.

The little mirror didn't seem to have any effect on the tentacle. Was she supposed to hit the darkenwraith in the face? But the creature's face was several metres away, hissing at a large, armoured man that Kasir was busy painting in the air.

Pallantu and Korak stood locked in close combat, and Edvin was getting to his feet after destroying yet another shadow. "Edvin!" Julia shouted. Her little brother came rushing to her side and thrust his dagger into the tentacle, which released Julia with a shriek. Together they ran up the low steps, to the chest.

Julia reached for the lid – but then she hesitated. Was it really wise to take the Darkenstar out in the middle of the fight? She didn't know how to use it.

What if Korak got hold of it? Her dad had locked it up to keep it away from the darkenwraiths, after all.

"Aren't you going to open it?" Edvin asked.

She shook her head. "I think we have to win first," she said.

"That might be hard without the Darkenstar," said Edvin.

Kasir now stood behind a wall of light grey warriors in armour, but several shadows were pressing hard against his defences. Pallantu was rolling on the floor with Korak, a tangle of white and black and flashing blue light.

"Come on," said Julia. "We have to help Pallantu."

She saw how Edvin tensed.

"You can do this," Julia said, smiling encouragingly. "See how many times you've defeated him now? And now we're going to work together." She felt the familiar warmth spread from her to Edvin. He stood straighter. "Come on – we can handle this." She led her little brother towards the rolling mass of black and white.

A shadow turned aside from the assault on Kasir to try to stop them, but the young prince threw a net from behind his defences, and the monster fell writhing to the ground at their feet. Julia struck the darkenwraith in the face with her mirror, and the creature roared and curled up, shrinking. The face was absolutely the right place to aim. Edvin finished the shadow off with a thrust to the chest, and they continued towards Pallantu and Korak.

"What are you doing, girl?" Pallantu gasped as the darkenwraith pressed him to the floor. "You were supposed to fetch the Darkenstar!"

"You don't need the Darkenstar to beat him, Pallantu," said Julia. "You're Paradisum's greatest creator, Pallantor's defender, Thousandworld's leading expert on how to defeat the darkenwraiths!"

Korak growled, suddenly struggling to hold the fallen creator down. Pallantu began to glow with a blue light that grew gradually stronger.

Julia seized the opportunity. "You're nothing, Korak!" she cried, swinging the mirror at the darkenwraith's head.

Korak was fast, but the mirror still grazed his head. The dark creature roared with pain. Then he was thrown off Pallantu in a sudden explosion of blue light and flew several metres back. Edvin ran after him and thrust the silver dagger into his black, shapeless belly.

Korak roared, seized Edvin in his tentacles and threw him aside roughly.

"Edvin!" Julia cried as her little brother hit the wall. She threw herself at the fallen darkenwraith, but a forest of dark tentacles rose against her, and she hesitated.

Then the tentacles were caught in a huge, light grey net. Korak struggled and twisted, but net after net fell over him as Kasir came striding forward with an expression of pure wrath on his face. Korak's shadows, which had held him in the corner, were now gone.

Meanwhile, Edvin was rising to his feet. He approached Korak unsteadily with the dagger in his hand. A dark tentacle rose against him, but he thrust the dagger into it, and it disappeared.

"I have to hold him," Kasir said, continuing to paint nets with desperate speed. "You must finish him off."

Julia fell to her knees and pressed the mirror to the darkenwraith's shapeless face. "You're nothing, Korak," she said. "Nothing!"

Korak screamed and shrank and tried to slither away, but Kasir held him fast in the nets. Then Edvin came and thrust the silver dagger deep into the darkenwraith's chest, and with a last roar, he was gone.

"We did it," Julia gasped. "We did it! Pallantu, we …" She turned towards the lanky creator, who lay groaning on the floor. She rushed to his side.

"You're strong, Pallantu," she said. "Strong and healthy and ready for anything. You must have some kind of trick that can help you now."

The man sat up with a groan, pulled a small glass bottle from his pocket and swallowed its contents in a single gulp. He sighed deeply. "I will survive," he said. "Now go and bring me the Darkenstar."

Julia hurried to the chest, placed her hands on the beautiful lid and lifted it. The chest opened as if the lock did not exist. The inside was lined with red velvet, and in the shadows at the bottom lay the Darkenstar.

The terrible weapon was a pitch-black ball, slightly larger than Julia's fist. She hesitated. It looked like part

270

of a darkenwraith, and the thought of touching it was incredibly unappealing.

"Bring it to me," said Pallantu. "Quickly! We have to take it and leave this place!"

Julia steeled herself and took the Darkenstar. It was cool but did not freeze her bones as the darkenwraith's attacks had. It didn't make her weak in the same way either. On the contrary, she felt a peculiar power filling her hands, an unpleasant, dirty power that reminded her of the dark words the guards on the drawbridge had spoken. She hurried towards Pallantu with the black ball. She didn't want to hold it for too long.

Suddenly Kasir stood in her way. "No," he said.

Julia stared. "Kasir," she said. "I have to give it to Pallantu."

"I cannot allow that," he said firmly. "The Darkenstar is too dangerous for a human to wield."

"Your Highness, think of your people," said Pallantu. "With this weapon, I can save your domain! Sulallia can be yours again!"

Kasir turned to the fallen creator and shook his head. "The Council entrusted the Darkenstar to Sulallia's royal family, to make sure that no one tried to use it. It is not yours to take, Pallantu. As prince of Sulallia, I say that Pallantu may not have the Darkenstar." He turned to Edvin. "Destroy it."

"Don't be a fool, Edvin," said Pallantu. "The fates of many worlds hang on this weapon. Think of your father! He wanted the Darkenstar kept safe until the day it could be used."

"And my mother wanted to destroy it," said Kasir. "If the Council had listened to her, then Sulallia would never have fallen. Destroy it, Edvin. Pallantu's word is not law in this domain."

Edvin looked in panic from Kasir to Pallantu, then to Julia. She didn't know what to do either, but she didn't want to hold the Darkenstar a single second longer.

A movement in the corner of her eye caught her attention, and she looked up and saw that one of the double doors was now open. There was no one there. The five-sided room was still empty, apart from herself, Edvin, Kasir and Pallantu – and the thrones and the chest, and the six statues of the artists standing in the middle of the floor.

She shook her head. "Kasir," she said. "Pallantu is the one who knows the most about the Darkenstar."

"Not more than my parents," the young prince said firmly.

Suddenly Julia was blinded by a flash of blue light. When her sight returned, she found herself on the floor along with Kasir and Edvin. Pallantu stood over them with the black ball clutched in his black hand. "Enough empty words and foolishness," he said. "It is time for me to see what this weapon can do." He raised the Darkenstar and laughed a horrible, threatening laugh. His eyes, which Julia had once thought resembled sapphires, were now as black as coal.

30

"What are you doing?" Julia said, horrified.

Pallantu turned his black gaze on her. "Saving the world, of course," he said. "But let us see now … how does this delectable creation work? It does not feel quite as I expected. It feels … better. Ah, now I see."

He held the Darkenstar in both hands, and a black beam shot out of it and struck Kasir in the chest. Kasir screamed and writhed on the floor.

"Stop!" Julia cried. She struggled to her feet, but then she too was struck by the black beam and collapsed in a heap.

Edvin rushed to her defence but was knocked down by a single word from Pallantu.

Slowly Julia stopped writhing as the pain faded into a cold and terrify feeling of weakness. This was uncannily similar to one of the darkenwraiths' attacks.

"Ah, so this is how that feels," Pallantu said, standing straighter. "You have so much potential – and now I have it!"

"Pallantu."

The dark beam disappeared at once, and Pallantu's gaze darted to and fro. "Lars-Petter?" he said, confused. It was the Troubadour's voice that had spoken.

Julia raised her tired head but did not see the Troubadour anywhere in the room. Only Edvin and Kasir lying on the ground with her, Pallantu standing over them, and the six statues in the middle of the floor.

"Pallantu," the Troubadour's voice said again. "Think about what you're doing. You're not yourself."

"And what would you know about that?" Pallantu shot back. He began stalking around the room, searching the five walls and the ceiling. He didn't appear to see any sign of the Troubadour either.

Lars-Petter sighed. "I know that you want power, Pallantu. And I'm ready to give you the power that I have. But you have to let the children go."

Pallantu laughed. "And what power can you offer me, Lars-Petter, now that I have the Darkenstar? Now that I can take all the power I want?"

"Knowledge," said Lars-Petter. "I can tell you about what happened when we took the Darkenstar in Trikonium. The day Angelica died. I can tell you what happened when I wielded the Darkenstar. I'm probably the only living person who's ever used it, aside from you."

Pallantu stiffened. "Have you used the Darkenstar?" he asked. "I have never heard that."

In the corner of her eye, Julia saw Edvin start to rise. "Wait," she whispered. He gave her a quizzical look but lay down on the floor again.

"No living person has ever heard my story," said the Troubadour. "But I will tell you everything – if you just wait and listen."

Julia glanced at Kasir and saw that he was awake but looked weak. His eyes were fixed on a certain spot in the middle of the room, and at once Julia understood. She waved at him to look away.

And then the Troubadour began his song. A sudden strumming of lute strings brought with it a feeling like rain on a beautiful cemetery. When Lars-Petter raised his voice and began to sing, Julia saw the whole scene in front of her.

Trikonium was a world that the shadow had taken, but not completely – the shadow had needed a human element, a stroke of artistic genius, to create the Darkenstar. It was Sindallus, a thinker, a matchless inventor, whom the darkenwraiths had used to design their terrible weapon.

The Council knew of the danger, and the Council sent the Three: Angelica, Henrik and Lars-Petter. The Three who travelled from world to world. The Three From Outside.

The Darkenstar was not yet perfected. The weapon was kept under guard until its completion, and the guards were terrible: nameless darkenwraiths, the likes of which had not been seen in any other domain.

Nevertheless, the Three managed to sneak in, defeat the guards and take the weapon. Lars-Petter took the black orb in his hand while Henrik and Angelica kept watch. They called for him – Angelica called, and he realised that he stood frozen. He felt the Darkenstar, and the Darkenstar felt him. He was filled with the Darkenstar's power, and the Darkenstar was filled with his power, and the Darkenstar was complete.

Lars-Petter knew that he could destroy every darkenwraith in Trikonium if he could only get more time. His friends called for him and he called for time. The Darkenstar whispered its mysteries, and he listened.

There he stood preparing himself when the darkenwraiths' reinforcements came. But the Darkenstar prepared itself as well. When he raised it to annihilate the enemy, it lowered his arms and formed words on his lips: "Take it! It is yours." He held the weapon out for the enemy to take.

It was Angelica who saved him. She and Dawn knocked the Darkenstar from his hand and she threw it to Henrik, who stuck it into a sack.

The enemy were too many, a whole world against the Three. They fled to the portal and reached it, barely.

Angelica was halfway through when the enemy took her. Dawn wailed.

"It was Henrik who came up with the version we told the Council," said the Troubadour. "He wanted to protect me. But he couldn't protect me from myself. That was when I left the Council and disappeared. And now you understand the danger of the Darkenstar."

"Now I understand much," said Pallantu. "Never before did I realise what a pitiful failure you are, Lars-Petter. I thought you took the blame for Angelica's death because you should have been faster, or stronger, or something like that. Never would I have dreamed that it was you who killed her. You who gave in to the darkness and extinguished her light."

"Don't listen to him!" Julia shouted. "It wasn't you, it was the darkenwraiths! It was the Darkenstar!"

Pallantu continued, taking no notice of her. "I understand that you are trying to warn me because you believe that you and I are alike, that I am as weak as you, that the Darkenstar could manipulate me into doing something against my will. But you do not understand, Lars-Petter – this is my will. And you cannot fool me. The king and queen may have liked you – but not enough to have *two* statues of you in the same room!"

A black beam shot out of the Darkenstar and struck a statue of the Troubadour holding a lute. The statue became the real, live Troubadour, and he fell to the floor with a cry.

"You have never been my equal, Lars-Petter," Pallantu said, striding towards the fallen, groaning Troubadour.

Now Julia felt strong again. It was almost as if the Troubadour's song, despite its sorrow, had in some way filled her with new strength. But what could she do?

Kasir acted first. He hurled a grey net that struck Pallantu and burst against his white-clad back. The black beam disappeared, and the man turned towards the young prince in irritation. "I suppose I shall have to take your power first, Your Highness," he said with an ironic bow.

Two high notes pierced the air, and Julia looked up and found to her surprise that it was the Troubadour who sang.

"Is that all the strength you have left, Lars-Petter?" Pallantu asked. "Two meaningless notes, accomplishing nothing? A final failed creation from a failed creator? I almost pity you."

The Troubadour smiled weakly. "Sometimes it's not about my strength," he said.

At that moment, one of the great windows shattered, and shards of glass cascaded over the stone floor. Pallantu turned in shock towards the window, just in time to be hit in the waist by a flying deer. He was knocked flat, and the black globe flew out of his hand and rolled away.

Julia rose and pounced on the Darkenstar. "Edvin!" she cried. "Destroy it!" She rolled the black orb to her little brother, who was now on his feet.

Pallantu shouted a word that made the air vibrate, and Edvin froze as if turned to stone. But then the Troubadour played a mighty chord on his lute, and the boy woke to life again.

Edvin fell to his knees and buried the silver dagger in the Darkenstar. The dark ball shrunk into nothing and vanished.

"You fool!" Pallantu screamed. He threw the winged deer off himself, rose to his feet and strode towards Edvin, his gaze burning. His eyes were hard sapphires. "You have squandered our only chance!" he cried. He raised his black hand, and it glowed with blue light.

His attack was caught by a grey wall from Kasir. When Pallantu turned to deal with the young prince, Julia got close enough to strike him in the back of the head with the mirror. It was probably a very foolish thing to do, since he wasn't a darkenwraith, but it was the best she could think of.

It seemed to help. Pallantu roared, clutching the back of his head as he turned to face her – but then he was knocked down by the winged deer once again. The Troubadour borrowed two brushes from Kasir and began to sing a song that made the room vibrate with power as they worked together to paint Pallantu into a grey cocoon.

The mighty speaker of the Council opened his mouth to say something, but the Troubadour painted over his mouth. Then, with a muffled cry of frustration, Pallantu disappeared in a flash of blue.

Julia blinked. "Is he …?"

The Troubadour shook his head. "No, he's alive. One of his rings has the power to transport him back to his tower. He's probably there now."

"You saved us," said Julia.

He avoided her gaze. "You saved me. After what you told me yesterday, I couldn't drink that wine. Your words made it taste like the poison it is. So I spat it out and started thinking instead. And then when His Highness came and found me last night and gave me back the lute and told me about your upcoming journey, I had a lot more to think about. Somehow I found hope. I went and woke the craftsman who was working on Dawn. I played for her as she used her talent, and it worked. That was probably what convinced me – when I saw Dawn, alive and clean again, free of the shadow."

"Convinced you of what?" asked Edvin.

"That the light really can defeat the darkness," said the Troubadour. "In Thousandworld, and in me."

"So she's alive," Julia said, amazed. She threw her arms around Dawn's neck, and the winged deer licked her face.

"She's alive," said the Troubadour. "But we have to get out of here, and quickly! A lot has happened here – the darkenwraiths will feel it in the air. They're probably on their way to investigate."

"Where will we go?" Edvin asked worriedly.

The Troubadour took up his lute. "Just stay close to me," he said. "I'll play silence and invisibility over us. At least I'll do my best."

"Your best will be more than enough," Julia said with a smile. "You're a brilliant creator."

31

The Troubadour's playing was enough to get them out of the palace, over the drawbridge, through the garden and back to the portal yard.

"This must really be a good lute," he said, stopping by a portal stone that looked like a large hand. He looked at the instrument in appreciation as he played it. "Quintonius was a master of his craft."

"And so are you," said Julia. "And so is Kasir, who fixed it."

"What about me?" said Edvin.

"You too," Julia said, tousling his hair. "You destroyed the Darkenstar." She smiled. Their victories were, in fact, hers.

"But I couldn't have done it without you," Edvin said. "I wouldn't have managed anything without you."

The Troubadour cleared his throat. "Not that I don't like to stand here playing silence and invisibility," he said. "But this domain is still full of darkenwraiths, and they're looking for us. It's probably time for me to take the three of you home to Klippsby. After I've sent Dawn back to Paradisum. She wouldn't get on well here, and in Klippsby she would just be a statue."

"Not," Kasir said suddenly. "Not Klissby."

He hadn't said a word since Pallantu had disappeared, and Julia was shocked to hear his accent again. She had become so used to thinking of him as an intelligent, confident young prince. Though she could still think of him that way, she reminded herself. Even if he sounded different, he was still the same person on the inside. She herself probably didn't sound particularly intelligent when she tried to speak Sulallian.

"Aren't you going back to Klippsby, Your Highness?" the Troubadour asked. "Didn't you want to rest from all the politics in Pallantor, rest from all the expectations, see a new world? Everything you told me last night?"

Kasir shook his head. "Pallantor," he said. "Must talk Council. Council must know. Korak gone. Darkenstar gone. Sulallia ..." He whistled something. "Mum here ... maybe. Maybe. Pallantu bad. Council must know." He said a few words in Sulallian.

The Troubadour nodded. "I understand. You're very brave, taking this upon yourself. This could mean many difficult conversations with the Council in the future. And now you have Pallantu as your enemy. The Darkenstar's effect on him should wear off soon. But even as his normal self, he's not going to appreciate you ruining his plan."

Kasir answered something incomprehensible in Sulallian.

"All right," said the Troubadour. "It's your decision, Your Highness. But then I'll have to send Dawn with you as an honour guard. And I'll come back to Pallantor to help you – as soon as I've spoken with their mother."

"Are you going to talk to Mum?" Edvin asked, his eyes wide. "But she thinks you're a disgusting drunk, and—"

Julia shushed him.

"Yes, I thought so too for a while," said the Troubadour. "But she knows who I really am, and now I know it too. And now you know who you are, even though she tried to keep it a secret from you for so many years. It's probably time to explain a few things to her. And time for her to explain a few things to you. But come – stay close to me. I have to send His Highness through the portal." He led them to a statue that looked like an enormous flower bulb, just like the one that had brought them to Paradisum from Maja's world.

"Wait!" said Julia. "Does this mean we're never going to see Kasir again? Or Dawn? Or you, after you drop us off?"

The Troubadour shook his head and laughed gently. "I said that I needed to talk to your mother," he said. "Now you know who you are – but I intend to make sure that you find out who you can *become*."